CW00496138

Geraldine's Taken

Clea Jones

Published by Vital Books Inc, 2023.

This is a work of fiction. Similarities to real people, places, or events are entirely coincidental.

GERALDINE'S TAKEN

First edition. September 9, 2023.

Copyright © 2023 Clea Jones.

ISBN: 979-8223358756

Written by Clea Jones.

Also by Clea Jones

CHAPTER ONE

GERALDINE

Geraldine woke up exactly one minute before the alarm clock rang.

She groaned... *5.29 a.m*... and reached out and slammed down on the clock before it had a chance to ring.

She'd been getting up early her whole life. *Half past five.* It was time to roll out of bed and get dressed for work.

She kicked the covers off and jumped out of her warm nest and had a good long graceful stretch— for five foot eleven she was supple and athletic—but her feeling of irritation refused to be shrugged off.

Geraldine loved the morning. She was a morning person. It wasn't the ungodly hour that made her groan. It wasn't even her job and the early start it forced on her that made her feel rebellious this morning.

She enjoyed running Helga's Seaside Antiques And Curios, and Helga's Seaside Guest House, even though it was really two jobs not one. Helga was a tough boss. She paid low wages and demanded total commitment. Helga ought to have employed two separate manageresses, one for the shop, and one for the guest house, but Geraldine didn't mind doing both jobs at once, even though it meant having to get up so early.

She'd always enjoyed a challenge. She didn't even mind the unpaid overtime. Geraldine liked taking responsibility, and there was plenty of that, particularly running the antiques side of Helga's business. Helga left it completely up to her to buy whichever pieces of Victorian furniture or nineteenth century jewelry she thought would sell in the shop. Geraldine had a good eye for antiques, particularly jewelry.

Everyone said Geraldine worked too hard, but she didn't resent the fact that Helga lived the high life up in New York, a thousand miles away, mixing with artists and celebrities, while she slaved away down here in Clifton paying for Helga's lavish lifestyle.

No. The reason Geraldine groaned this morning, the reason she felt unusually rebellious, wasn't her job or jealousy of Helga.

... The reason was hanging on the back of her bedroom door...

... Ostentatious enough to make any girl want to kick over the traces, a flamboyant and blatant joke at her expense...

... a Gilded Age evening dress...

... *A* genuine fin-de-siècle party gown replete with pearl bead-work bodice in blue satin, cinched waist and ankle-length skirt bulked out by God knows how many petticoats *that she was supposed to wear today...*

It was hard to tell if Helga was serious or just wished to humiliate her. Helga was catty enough to make her underlings dress up to look ridiculous, especially if that underling was Geraldine. Geraldine had an idea her boss was jealous of her statuesque, curvy figure, pretty face and stunning auburn hair.

The fact that the strapless gown was pretty revealing, meant to show off a Gilded Age belle's 'embonpoint' only made it worse.

Helga had had the brilliant idea of having a 'Gilded Age Week' — *she expected her to wear the dress for seven freaking days!*— to promote the nineteenth century antiques, curios and jewelry sold in the shop and the nineteenth century décor of the guest house.

The whole staff was supposed to dress in period costume.

Beth, who helped in the guest house, as an eighteen-eighties chambermaid.

Diane, who part-timed in the kitchen, as ye Olde Worlde cook.

And Geraldine's boyfriend, Greg, who did all the maintenance and was never out of a pair of oily overalls, as a nineteenth-century artisan. Apparently Gilded Age artisans wore smocks and knee breeches. Greg had already said Helga could go f*** herself.

Geraldine could just picture her boss, a thousand miles away in her Manhattan penthouse in her chic business suits with her arty friends, having a good snigger at 'dear Geraldine' in her 'stunning' evening gown. She was going to be the laughing stock of Clifton for the next seven days.

Geraldine yawned and gave her shoulders a good flex. She rumpled her thick auburn hair.

She took the dress down from its hanger on the back of the door, held it against her body and looked in the mirror.

No. Really. Greg was right. Helga could go f*** herself.

It was so unfair! She had the sort of statuesque build and shapely curves that look good in slacks, miniskirts, decolleté cocktail frocks, tank tops, short shorts... *anything* except this piss-taking fancy-dress. She didn't mind a scoop-neck bodice, even a *low* scoop-neck bodice—she had a nice cleavage— *but with puff shoulders?*

Her eyes flashed in the mirror. With her green eyes, high cheekbones and the bronze glint in her auburn mane, her face looked good when she was angry.

No. It was all very well for Greg. She was the one who'd have to tell Helga to go f*** herself if Helga turned up out of the blue, or, more likely, if one of the guests or customers turned out to be a spy. Helga was quite capable of sending people down to the shop to keep an eye on her. Helga was also quite capable of sacking her on the spot after five years' conscientious hard work, if her slightest whim was ignored.

No. She loved Clifton. She had a good life in this little seaside village, even if she felt unsatisfied at times.

She slipped out of her nightie, clipped on a bra and thrust her head into a swamp of petticoats. Her hair snagged in gauzy layers of tulle. She couldn't see. She eventually found the waistband, thrust her head and arms through, located the shoulder puffs, got her hands free and with a massive sigh shrugged the bodice down over her breasts.

In spite of all expectations the gown fitted her. Helga knew her size. The bead-work gathered up her breasts in a tight pearl net. She was slim enough for the cinched waist. She battered the skirts and petticoats into a semblance of a Gilded Age crinoline.

Now there were just a couple of hundred pearl buttons to do up at the back. The dress was made for ladies with maids, not pissed off shop manageresses.

She pushed the last little disk through the final tiny hole.

Finally.

She looked in the mirror.

She looked ridiculous. It was the sort of gown sallow maidens sat sighing at their casement windows in, waiting for some dark-eyed, dashing gentleman to come along and sweep them off their feet. And who did she have?

Greg.

Greg was okay. In fact Greg was more than okay. A blonde-haired seaside hunk. A kind heart to go with the ripped physique. Not much in the way of ambition except for getting married to Geraldine. Greg was a lovely guy, but hardly a dark-eyed, dashing gentleman.

All the other girls in Clifton envied her going out with Greg. He really was gorgeous. She'd sort of half agreed to his marriage proposals. He was thoughtful and caring. He'd be great with kids. He'd make a good husband but more and more often lately Geraldine had caught herself rebelling against Greg too, not just Helga.

In fact she'd started dreaming of a man— not necessarily dark-eyed, she couldn't even picture him— *who'd take her*. Yes. That was the word, *take*, like a piece of jewelry off a shelf, so she could sparkle with love like a diamond without even having to think about whether she was in love or not. A thief who'd take her and flaunt her high-colored beauty for his own prestige, and sunny, good-natured Greg certainly wasn't anything like that.

And now this ridiculous gown of Helga's and...

... Oh God!...

... She'd totally forgotten...!

... She was due at Portslade in half an hour...!

... The old lady—she'd sounded extra old over the phone— had insisted on a ridiculously early hour... to look over a batch of jewelry she was selling off...

... She needn't have put on her Gilded Age debutante's dress till she got back from Portslade and opened the shop and she didn't have time to change into something more comfortable now...

... The old lady had sounded crotchety over the phone, one of those old dears who are ultra picky about punctuality...

Geraldine freshened up her face, slipped on a pair of trainers—the skirt brushed the floor, there was no need to worry about heels—gathered up her crinoline, and made a dash for it.

Her car was parked round the back of the shop.

Thank God.

Greg was there.

Greg could drive her. Gilded Age debs don't drive either. They don't freaking do anything. Not with pearl and satin bodices and three hundred buttons choking the life out of them.

Greg was in his workshop working on his motorbike. He put down his spanner.

"Wow! Look at you!"

Christ! How could she have ever imagined she was getting bored of him?

Even in a pair of oily overalls Greg was a hunk, big and beefy and clever with his hands too. He was reconditioning a sixties Harley Davison. The bike was going to be a masterpiece of automative restoration if he ever got it finished.

"La Belle Dame Sans Merci!"

His eyes feasted on her, appreciatively or mockingly she couldn't quite tell.

"La who?"

No. He was laughing at her.

"'Belle dame sans merci.' The beautiful lady without pity!"

Greg was clever too, as well as good looking. He liked poetry. 'The beautiful lady without pity' was no doubt from some old romantic poem.

Geraldine laughed.

"The beautiful lady without pity? I feel more like a tailor's dummy!"

"No seriously..." said Greg. He gave her a long appraising survey. "... You look wonderful..."

He wiped his hands on his overalls and grabbed her. His big muscular arms wrapped around her and drew her close. She'd been busy this week. They hadn't slept together for a few nights. She could feel his cock stiffening already in his overalls.

She let him kiss her. She enjoyed feeling the power she had over him, his dick getting harder and harder as he crushed her in his arms. Five years going steady and Greg still boned up quick. It made her discontent crowd in on her even more disturbingly.

"... Stop it, Greg... not now...*no!*... I've got to be at Portslade in twenty minutes... to look at Mrs Daley's jewelry..."

He let go of her and wiped his hands on his overalls again.

"Portslade? I'll drive you." She didn't even have to ask. "La Belle Dame Sans Merci always has a chauffeur!"

She laughed. Greg was funny too. It wasn't his fault that he no longer reduced her to a swamp of molten need like he used to.

"Good! I sure feel like being chauffeured."

CHAPTER TWO

GERALDINE

Greg drove a VW Beetle— another vehicle he'd reconditioned himself. The VW had been his years long-project before the Harley Davison.

The seats had a nice plastic smell. He'd renewed the upholstery and replaced the steering wheel and gear-stick with forty-five model originals.

You could feel the power of the hotted up engine growling through the floor.

They sped along the cliff road in crisp, fresh sunlight.

Big cliffs towered above them on one side of the road, with a sheer two-hundred-foot drop beyond the crash barrier on the other. Greg was a fast, decisive driver, but even his flashy driving bored her now.

She wanted more than speed, she wanted to be taken out of herself. She didn't want to be impressed by a hotted up VW and a good driver, she needed a love that would sweep her away, maybe even annihilate her. And here she was stuck in a freaking Gilded Age gown a hundred and fifty years out of style because chic, New York bitch Helga thought it would sell antiques.

"Seriously. You look great, Geraldine. That dress does something for you."

Greg was trying to be nice, but he was only getting on her nerves more and more.

"Yeah," she said. "It does something for me. It makes me sick to my stomach."

She had a hot body, hotter than Helga's, and it was being buried alive in satin and pearls and ankle-length silk.

"No. Really..." said Greg. "... It brings out something in you..." He took his eyes off the road for a split second to look her up and down again. "... Something real hot..."

She didn't even bother to answer. Five years ago, when they'd first met, drives along the cliffs like this had been exciting. She and Greg had done some pretty wild things in the past. Wild and romantic. She'd felt alive and free back then. He licked his lips:

"… Yeah… a man could get to fancy him some hot Gilded Age babe…"

Now they were just like any other couple, arranging the next time they'd have sex as if it were a doctor's appointment or something.

She grabbed the wheel.

She thrust the wheel left. Tires slewed sideways into the oncoming lane. Greg hit the brakes.

"Geraldine!"

Towering stone screeched towards them.

Greg managed to get control and steered his precious VW into niche of hard shoulder carved out of the cliff face.

"What the hell?"

She slipped her hand in through the hips of his overalls, gouged hairy muscle under hot elastic and grabbed his dick.

"GERALDINE!"

He was nice. He was more than nice. He'd just had the shock of his life, she'd nearly totaled his precious VW, and his cock was rock-hard.

She laughed in his face.

"Fancy some Belle Dame Sans Merci?"

She unclipped his bib—overalls suited Greg, especially with his big penis rearing out of the oily denim—overalls suited him more than Gilded Age couture suited her.

She slid his pounding piston down her throat like a meaty sword into its slippery scabbard. She gargled his swollen tip in sweet throat honey, impaled some Adam's apple on his throbbing spear-head.

"… Argh…"

I'm not freaking Helga's plaything, alright?

"… Argh… argh…"

I'm hotter than Helga, okay?
"... Argh... glurg... gla-aaarg..."
I'm beautiful.

Good old Greg. He always stepped up to the plate. His dick was always on stand-bye, rock-hard in an instant. Never stopping loving her. Packed vein and pulsing gristle for her to retch up all the beauty and love and daring she had inside her on. He groaned:

"I thought you had to meet this old lady!"

She drew her mouth away trailing strings of grateful gag.

"She can wait."

His fingers were in her hair savoring its russet luster, guiding her mouth back down where he needed it more than words.

"Fuck, Geraldine..."

"... Argh... argh... argh-lllllllllllllll..."

She was alive. She was strong and beautiful. She wasn't some boring drone at the mercy of pernickety old ladies and chic chicks like Helga.

A car streamed past.

She clamped his pulsing shaft with her teeth way down deep and raked a sweet love-bite upwards—God how nice and big he was!—nipped a ridge of slippery tip, spread some pre-cum round on throbbing tightness with the tip of her tongue.

"You know what a nice cock you've got, Greg?"

He mumbled something incoherent. No, he didn't know. Not really.

"I want it inside me, alright? I need your big cock deep inside me. I want you to fuck my brains out. *Now!*"

They hadn't spoken to each other like that for a long time.

"Here?"

He was so nice.

The VW was poky. It was hard getting the dress up around her hips, it had so many freaking petticoats.

Silk hissed. Tulle rustled. Petticoats got snagged on the forties gear stick. By the time she got the skirts gathered up high enough there was so much petticoat bunched around her waist, she couldn't see what she was doing, only feel the sharp heat aching between her legs.

She pulled her panties to one side and tried to straddle him

Her bottom banged the steering wheel. There wasn't enough room. Greg just sat there, in pole position on some dazed grid. She couldn't get her body between the wheel and his muscly singlet.

"Shift the seat back, can't you?"

He reached down and a lever thumped and the seat jolted backwards and she climbed over his tall dick in an avalanche of silk and satin and pearl. They kissed. She battened on his strong broad mouth, plastered desperate heat on his lovely lips, tongues grappling like they'd only just met.

She didn't even need to guide him in. His swollen tip was tight as a drum, drumming its own sweet beat into her molten surrender, ticking for her and her alone as her yearning swamp sank down onto it.

"... Oh... oh... oh God...!"

She surrendered inch after inch onto his pounding piston, jerking and bucking in luscious abandon before she even hit rock bottom.

"... Oh... oh... yes... yes..."

A semi trailer roared past, its slip stream rocking the VW.

Strong palms cupped her bottom, fed its helpless jerking onto his pulsing stake. There was a smell of oil. Greg always had oil in his fingernails but it wasn't a problem. His hands told her how sumptuous her ass was, exploring her tight cleft, squeezing like crazy.

"... Yes... yes... fuck me, Greg... please fuck me..."

His hands slid up her back picking at buttons, unfastening some, failing at others—there were too many freaking buttons— strong fingers slid under her armpits—her puffed shoulders were around her elbows, he was going to tear them— and closed round her breasts, crushed helpless bra cup into her voluptuous softness, palmed hot taut nipple, reining her in, her pussy rutting helplessly on his gorgeous dick.

"I love you, Geraldine."

His cock convulsed, deep inside her.

"... I love you too, Greg.."

She could feel it. The deep affection he felt for her. The love that would last a lifetime. Tensed need letting go. He was cumming.

"... Take me... I want you to take me..."

He loved her. He made a superhuman effort. His body clenched. Strong fingers gouged breasts. It hurt. He stopped himself from cumming. He wanted to give her more pleasure. He managed to keep himself from climaxing. He always did.

The pleasure began. They began to move in sync. The rocking of her hips matched the sweet surges of his cock up into her. Her butt undulated lifted on the steady weight of his thrusts.

Their bodies rocked as one, the tide of love beginning to carry them away. She was going to be very late seeing her old lady.

It always happened like this. Greg nearly cumming too quickly, but managing to control himself for her sake, and then the long slow ebb and flow towards a shared climax.

She glanced at the clock on the dashboard.

Jesus Christ! It was quarter past eight already!

Oh God! Her appointment was for eight, and they were only halfway to Portslade! Stock buying negotiations always took a long time and then she was supposed to be back in Clifton by nine to open the shop!

Geraldine felt her pussy clutch, that special squeeze that they both knew, deep inside her, and the next instant they were rutting, two animals in heat, fucking like crazy, going over the brink together.

"... Yes... oh God... yes... ye-eeeeeeeeeeeeeeeeees...!"

Her hot gash jerked and bucked as Greg filled it with warm generous love, so warm and generous it was trickling down her inner thighs before he'd even finished unloading and mixing with her own creamy juice.

She quickly climbed off him.

"Thank you, baby. That was great." She found some tissues in the glove compartment and cleaned herself up. "We'd better get a move on."

She smoothed her petticoats down and straightened her bodice.

The engine was still running. Greg pulled out into the rush hour traffic.

He drove the rest of the way even faster.

Geraldine sat back and enjoyed the ocean slipping by hundreds of feet below, the tall crags flashing by far overhead. She felt better, much more relaxed, but a gnawing uncertainty still ate at her.

CHAPTER THREE

GREG

Swinging the VW round curve after curve, Greg felt confused.

He should have felt blissed out and fulfilled. He *was* blissed out. He *did* feel fulfilled. When a woman as fit as Geraldine comes onto you like that, you have no option but to feel on top of the world... and yet...

She could have killed them, grabbing the wheel like that. If there hadn't been a lay-bye in the rock-face they would have skidded into the cliff. And the way she'd straddled him! The urgency with which she'd fucked him! It was crazy. Something was preying on her mind.

They'd only made love like that, in crazy ways like that, years ago when they first met. He knew Geraldine loved him. She loved him as much as he loved her, but perhaps she was getting bored with him. She seemed restless. She wanted more excitement from their relationship.

No. That wasn't it. That wasn't the reason Geraldine was in a strange mood. *She wanted them to get married!* Yes. That was it. *Geraldine was getting impatient for him to propose to her!* Well. He'd been proposing to her for a couple of years now but she wanted him to be more assertive, *to demand that she marry him.* They'd been going out for five years. They both knew they'd spend the rest of their lives together and raise a family.

He'd enjoyed this impromptu love making, but something was wrong. Geraldine was getting broody. It was time for them to marry and settle down.

The lady with whom Geraldine had the appointment lived in a big, gloomy house overlooking the sea. At some time in the past it must have been a very grand house. It had big bay windows and even a turret for viewing the ocean, but now the bay windows were shuttered and the paint was peeling on the windowsills.

They pulled up outside the house. He said:

"I'll wait here."

"No. Come in with me."

She was in a weird mood. Perhaps it was the old-fashioned dress Helga had made her wear. Helga was a domineering boss. He'd met Helga a number of times himself, and if you asked him, Helga was jealous of how beautiful and attractive Geraldine was. She'd dreamed up this 'Gilded Age' so she could rub Geraldine's nose in her menial position.

Helga didn't even pay Geraldine properly for all the responsibility she took on, running the guest house on top of running the shop, and buying and valuing stock like she was doing now, in her own time.

They went up the front path together. Geraldine rang the bell.

As far as Greg was concerned, far from looking ridiculous, Geraldine looked superb in her old-fashioned gown. She looked like a wild, auburn-haired angel. The satin bodice clung nice and tight. The pearl bead-work followed every voluptuous curve and dip of her breasts. The long silk skirt might cover up her legs, but that just left more for the imagination to enjoy.

She smiled nervously and smoothed the skirt over her thighs. The three days they'd gone without sex had left her sticky.

The door creaked open. A pale face peered through the crack.

Geraldine put on her bright efficiency voice:

"Hello, Mrs Daley. It'm Geraldine. Geraldine MacGuire? From Seaside Antiques And Curios?"

"You're late!" snapped the grim old mouth.

"... Erm... well yes... I'm terribly sorry... I...erm..."

"Who's this?"

Watery eyes glared at Greg.

Geraldine's smile wavered.

"He's... erm... he's..." Her eyes brightened. "... Security!... you told me your jewelry was valuable. I brought my security guard!"

She gave him a quick grin. Geraldine was brilliant. She knew exactly how to handle difficult old ladies like this.

"He doesn't look like a security guard!"

"Oh," said Geraldine. "I assure you he is."

"Why isn't he wearing a uniform?"

The old biddy glared at his oily overalls.

Geraldine laughed.

"Oh, he's my... erm... he's my chauffeur too..."

Chains rattled. Bolts slid. Eventually the door opened.

The house smelled bad. The living room reeked of stale cooking oil and cat litter.

Mrs Daley disappeared into a darkened room and came out with a carrier bag. It was full of jewelry.

"I want a full inventory. You're not leaving with all these precious items without giving me a full inventory and receipt."

"Of course, Mrs Daley," said Geraldine. "I quite understand."

Geraldine peeked into the bag.

She gave Greg a quick, wry look out of the corner of her eye.

It was a load of tat. Mrs Daley's 'precious items' were all but worthless. They'd come all this way for nothing. The perished carrier bag was full of tawdry costume jewelry that had devalued from even its cheap cost sixty years ago. The whole lot would probably only fetch a hundred dollars in the shop if Mrs Daley was lucky.

Most manageresses would have told the old woman to keep her tat, and torn a strip off her for wasting their time. But not Geraldine. Geraldine sat down with a pen and pad and spread the jewelry out on the table and made a painstaking list of every single item.

Greg felt a surge of love for her. She wasn't just a beautiful face and a red hot body that climbed on top of you in cliff-side lay byes. Geraldine had a kind heart too. She possessed an honest nature that was even more generous than her sensational body. It was why Helga trusted her to manage the shop single handed. It was why people up and down the coast trusted Geraldine to value their jewelry and curios and sell them at a fair price.

"This is nice," said Geraldine, holding up a butterfly brooch covered with what were obviously fake diamonds. "It looks almost genuine..."

Her face flushed. She was even more beautiful when she blushed... blushing now at her slip of the tongue...

"Of course it's genuine!" snapped the old lady. "What do you mean 'almost'. It's Fabergé. That's what it is. That butterfly cost twenty thousand dollars in nineteen forty nine!"

The poor old thing. She wasn't just old and difficult, she was gaga.

"... Well..." said Geraldine. "... I'm afraid I can still only offer you two hundred dollars for the whole lot, Mrs Daley..."

Geraldine was so bighearted! She felt sorry for the old lady. There was no way the carrier bag full of old-fashioned rubbish was worth more than a hundred dollars, but she was trying to help Mrs Daley by offering her two hundred.

"Oh! Alright!" snapped the old lady. "It's highway robbery! But I'll take two hundred."

She knew when she was getting a good deal.

It was nine thirty before Geraldine finished making an inventory of all the jewelry in the carrier bag and had paid Mrs Daley her two hundred dollars.

Twenty thousand for the butterfly in nineteen-forty-nine but she was quick enough snatching the money out of Geraldine's hand.

"... Well thank you very much, Mrs Daley. It's been a pleasure doing business with you..."

She was going to be very late opening the shop this morning, but she never once hurried the old lady, even though it somehow always seemed to get back to Helga whenever the shop opened late. Nine thirty? Helga was going to come down on Geraldine like a ton of bricks.

Driving back along the cliff road Greg realized what a jewel he had in Geraldine. He'd always loved her, but this morning his heart was overflowing.

Yes. It was time to take her out somewhere nice— they hadn't been out much lately— a candlelit dinner and a bottle of champagne and ask her to be his wife.

CHAPTER FOUR

GREG

When they got back, Greg parked the VW round the back in the garages.

"Do you need some help?"

Before they even got out of the car it was clear that everything was in chaos.

Geraldine already looked frantic.

It was the first time he'd ever seen her truly overwhelmed by the number of responsibilities she had to juggle at one time.

It was nearly ten, and the shop still wasn't open.

Kirsty, the girl who helped Geraldine in the shop, hadn't turned up, or even bothered to ring and tell Geraldine she wasn't coming in.

A coach party of tourists had turned up to take advantage of Helga's Seaside Antiques And Curios 'Gilded Age' Promotion Week, and gone away grumbling. Geraldine's absence was sure to get back to Helga.

On top of the problems with the shop, Beth, the girl who helped run the guest house had been rude to one of the guests when they complained about their breakfast. Beth had been indignant at being made to wear a chambermaid's costume and she'd burned the toast and overcooked the eggs and bacon on purpose. He said:

"Is there anything I can do?"

Geraldine gave him a brusque kiss.

"No. I don't think so. Thanks."

"Love you," said Greg as she dashed off to open up the shop.

Greg headed for his garage. He'd do a bit of work on the Harley before he had a look at that busted boiler.

"Hi, Greg."

"*Ey?* What are you doing here?"

It was Beth, the girl who'd turned everything upside down in the guest house.

"Put that cigarette out!"

It was typical of Beth to be smoking where there were tins of oil and gasoline stored. Beth was a scrawny eighteen-year-old. She was sexy if you liked snaky hips and a slinky way of wiggling her bottom. Her snaky hips and slinky style sure looked funny in a maid's cap and frilly apron. He said:

"Why aren't you in the guest house, helping Geraldine?"

"Ah, Jeez, Greg." Beth pouted. "Give us a break. Dressin' us up like freaking Downton Abbey. Geraldine's taking the piss."

She stubbed her cigarette out and sidled over to the Harley. She draped herself over the seat.

"It's not Geraldine's idea," said Greg. "It's Helga's. Get off my bike."

The maid's dress was short. Beth perched herself across the bike. Jesus wept. She was making sure he got a glimpse of her panties. Make that thong.

"When'll you be finished the Harley Greg? I'm dyin' for a ride."

Greg took a deep breath. Not again. He was going to have to do something about Beth. At first, the way she'd played up to him had flattered his ego. Any thirty-year-old guy likes to think he still has pull with a hot teenager like Beth. But now, she was just irritating.

"Go and help, Geraldine," he said. "And apologize too."

Beth slid off the bike.

"Apologize for what?"

"You know what."

"Yeah. Alright. Sor-ee..."

She swayed against him as she walked past, her hip grazing the bulge in his overalls— God, what was wrong with him this morning?— and lingering there an instant.

GERALDINE

Geraldine put Mrs Daley's bagful of jewelry in the safe, and got to work.

It took her hours to get things sorted out.

She opened up and rang the tour company, and apologized for the shop being shut when the party of tourists came.

She promised special discounts on all items purchased and the coach party returned at lunch time and spent six hundred dollars on intaglio brooches, hair lockets, art nouveau pins and an imitation Lalique vase.

She arranged for back-up staff for the guest house. Beth emerged out of nowhere.

With a great deal of quiet diplomacy, and more discount rates, Geraldine managed to smooth the ruffled feathers of the guests. The one Beth had insulted had stormed off unfortunately. Room Fourteen, the Ocean View Suite, was going to be empty for a week at the busiest time of year.

Another black mark against her name.

Geraldine thought of docking Beth's wages, but the poor girl's wages were so low already she didn't have the heart.

By three o'clock everything was under control and— lo and behold!— Kirsty turned up.

Geraldine ought to have torn a strip off her for taking advantage, but by this time she was feeling too strung out to do it.

She'd missed lunch. At least she'd be able to have an hour to herself now.

She told Kirsty to take over.

"I'll be back in a while."

She headed for her bedroom and locked the door behind her.

She was having a bad day, in fact, a terrible day. There was something wrong with her. Usually work drove the mixed-up thoughts out of her head, the harder the work the more clearly she was able to think. But not today.

She took her Lucida Dream vibrator out of the drawer where it was hidden. She had a nice kind hunky man who loved her *why did she even need a freaking vibrator?*

It was crazy doing that with Greg by the side of the cliff highway. She could have killed the two of them grabbing the wheel like that. She'd climaxed—she could climax most of the time with Greg—and she still wasn't satisfied. She felt scared. True satisfaction starts in the heart.

She lay down on the bed and pulled her skirt up round her waist. She didn't have time to take it off.

She pulled her panties aside. She was wet. True fulfillment begins in the heart and she was being carted around by a slippery ache between her legs.

At the mere approach of the humming globe of smooth plastic frissons of ecstasy rippled her quaking depths. Not even ecstasy was enough.

"... Oh... oh..."

Greg's swollen tip, its sumptuous smear of pre-cum, couldn't fill her like her Lucida Dream filled her at even its first voluptuous touch—her clit went into spasm— filled the emptiness in her heart, melting pussy lips clutching at throbbing plastic like wet, burning clingfilm.

She switched the power up to maximum. Humming smoothness churned her clit.

"... Oh... oh... oh God...!"

Warm waves of pleasure flowed up her body, arched her back, lifted her belly in ecstasy.

The rounded tip— she tried to imagine it was Greg's, but the feeling wouldn't come— slithered in aching wetness and sank into her pussy. The curved shaft found her G-spot of its own accord, massaging the roof of her molten tunnel... but she still couldn't picture Greg... she was usually able to imagine Greg inside her when she masturbated, but today he was gone.

She wanted more than Greg's self restraint and affectionate skill. She wanted more than even fucking. She needed to be *taken*, taken body and soul.

Of its own accord, the vibrator slipped in deeper. The thing had a mind of its own. It set off spasms of delight all up and down her body, working its way into her quaking swamp, the sopping depths where she was alone. It wasn't enough. It would never be enough.

Dark brown eyes looked down at her. She knew they were only a picture in her head, but the dark lustrous irises seemed almost real. Dark and lustrous, and cold and ruthless. Probing, piercing. Seeing everything.

"... Yes... yes... oh God... yes... ye-eeeeees...!"

Her pussy clenched. Sopping depths clutched and let go. The waves of pleasure turned into a tsunami.

"... Yes... ye-eeeeeeeeeeeeeeeeeeeeeeeeeeeeeeees...!"

She writhed and bucked on the bed. She cried out her desperate plea as an ecstasy more powerful than anything she'd ever known, sweeter than she'd ever dreamed, swamped her.

CHAPTER FIVE

GERALDINE

Geraldine lay slumped on the bed, thinking that perhaps an hour or two's sleep would be a nice way to end this tiring day.

She was already drifting off when there was a knock at her door.

She hurriedly arranged her dress. Thank heavens she'd thought to lock her door.

"Yes?"

Beth's voice came through the door.

"It's me, miss. There's a man at reception wants to book a room."

Geraldine sighed.

"Can't you deal with it?"

Beth's voice came back.

"He wants to speak to the manageress."

"Show him the Ocean View Suite."

"I have. He still wants to speak to you."

For God's sake, you can book a room without speaking to the freaking manageress.

Geraldine climbed off the bed. She was never rude to customers but, good God, was she to get no peace?

She hurried through the shop and round to the reception counter of the guest house.

A tall, dark-haired man stood at the counter in a posture that clearly displayed impatience, even anger.

He looked up. His eyes met hers.

Geraldine's heart stopped beating. She was falling through the bottom of her stomach into an abyss.

His dark lustrous brown eyes took her in. They looked her up and down, imperiously, as if he owned her.

That his face was handsome, in a dark, saturnine way, she barely took in.

That his tall body was willowy and powerful in its expensive suit she could barely make out. All she saw were his eyes. His dark brown taking in every inch of her in, making every inch of her his own.

He cocked an eyebrow at the homely counter, the furniture, the décor.

"Are you the manageress?" He cast an eye over her dress. "Or am I speaking to another waitress?"

She couldn't breathe. His rudeness was appalling, but his eyes were the eyes she'd conjured climaxing on her vibrator. They were the eyes that had pushed her over the edge into the best orgasm she'd ever had, into an ecstasy better than anything she'd ever felt with Greg.

She gathered herself up, and said, as coldly as she could:

"I'm the manageress. How can I help you?"

His upper lip curled.

"Help me...?" His lips were broad and attractive. They were so sensuous she wanted to press her mouth to his mouth, even if it was sneering at her. His eyes slid to her throat and then to her breasts, straining at ribbed pearls, fluttering under blue satin. "... I could think of a number of ways."

It was too much. His impertinence was appalling.

She straightened her back, and said as forcefully as she could:

"You can think whatever you like, sir. Your thoughts are none of my business."

Her voice betrayed her. His thoughts *were* her business. She knew exactly what they were. He was thinking about which way he'd prefer to fuck her. The choice was his, not hers. He was thinking it in detail, maybe thrusting her face down onto the counter and lifting her skirt and taking her from behind, or maybe forcing her to her knees and jamming his lordly cock into her mouth. She was clairvoyant. She could see the thoughts moving around inside his head.

He smiled. His smile made her go weak at the knees.

"I want a room. I need a room for a few days." In a flash his voice was refined, almost gentle. As if, after ravishing her with his harshness he was caressing her hurt pride. "Do you have anything?"

His suit was breathtakingly expensive. He moved with a willowy sinuousness, but she could see that under the exclusive silk/merino weave his body was toned and buff and had a steely whip to it.

"A room?"

Her head spun. Thank God, they were booked out. This guy was too much. He'd destroy her in a single night—she was already yearning for a single night—there was something dangerous and destructive about him.

"No. I'm afraid, sir..." She remembered the guest who'd stormed out that morning, over Beth's rudeness. "... Well, actually..." She told herself to insist that they were full. She didn't have a room. He was already turning her world upside down. "... There is the Ocean View Suite. That's available at the moment. Though I'm sure..." She had to put up a fight. She needed to show him that she wasn't a pushover. "... I'm sure our Ocean View Suite will be much too humble for a gentleman of your pretensions."

There. That was a good hit. 'Pretensions'— it was exactly the word for him.

"I'll take it."

She felt so helpless he might as well have said 'you', as 'it.'

"... Erm... well... yes... okay... your name...?"

He leaned towards her as she opened the registry.

"Richard..."

"Just Richard...?" Christ. She needed to put up at least a bit of resistance. "... As in Coeur de Lion?"

She blushed to the roots of her hair. How stupid can you get? 'Coeur de Lion'? This guy was a real, in-the-flesh 'Lionheart', if she'd ever seen one.

"... Braughton," he said. "... Richard Braughton..."

She took down his details, ran his credit card through the machine, and handed him the key to his room.

"Second floor. The door on the left." She nodded at his Louis Vuitton luggage. "You'll be alright with that, will you?"

She wanted to fuck him so badly she didn't trust herself to show him up to his room.

"Yeah. Sure. I'll be fine."

One more swashbuckling smile, and he headed for the stairs.

RICHARD

Richard traveled light. His suitcase wasn't heavy at all. At the bend in the stairs he turned and looked back at her. She was bending over the registry filling in some last details, her auburn hair covering her face.

Helga had told him that Geraldine was an efficient and honest manageress. Helga hadn't mentioned that she was beautiful too.

CHAPTER SIX

GREG

Twenty four hours passed but Greg only felt more and more uneasy. Something bad was happening. Geraldine was in a weird mood, doing weird things. Even Beth was starting to disturb him.

He didn't fancy Beth. He didn't even like her, but when she'd waylaid him in the garage he had to admit he'd responded. Perched up on the Harley, a glimpse of thong under frilly apron, she'd got to him.

Beth was bad news. She was a little slut. She was lazy too. She let Geraldine down all the time. But when she'd brushed against him, brushed against him deliberately, as she walked out of the garage, his cock had stiffened. Not a lot, but it had stiffened enough to worry him.

He loved Geraldine. He loved Geraldine with all his heart. He'd made up his mind to ask her again to marry him, be more commanding this time. He felt pretty sure she'd say yes. They'd been going out for five years and now, and it had been five years of almost complete happiness and a steadily growing trust and companionship.

He didn't feel any real threat from Beth's direction. He wasn't even tempted.

Beth had been coming on to him for ages, and he'd always managed to brush her off with a joke or some friendly stupidity that didn't hurt her feelings. If she had any feelings, that is. No. He wasn't interested in Beth in the slightest, not when he had a woman like Geraldine, but Greg still felt disturbed.

Geraldine was in a funny mood. He'd never seen her so restless, or so unpredictable. He'd enjoyed it yesterday, fucking her in the car. Doing it out on the cliff road had been a buzz. But there was something about the way she'd climbed on top of him that hadn't felt right. She'd been so hungry and urgent.

They'd climaxed together. Everything had been okay, sort of. More than okay, but she'd still left him with the impression that he hadn't satisfied her.

He should have asked Geraldine to marry him years ago. That was where he'd gone wrong, not taking the leap and really insisting earlier on in their relationship. They were made for each other. Geraldine was twenty eight now. It was the age when a woman wants to settle down and have children.

He felt a sudden, crazy fear that he might lose her if he didn't do something immediately, something positive, straight away, to make her his forever.

She'd never even looked at another man. Not once, all the time they'd been going out. Neither had he looked at another woman. They'd both been one hundred percent faithful to one another. A little straycat like Beth was no competition for a classy woman like Geraldine. But Greg felt a sudden need to act. He had to make changes in the way he lived.

Starting with the way he dressed.

He looked down at his dirty, oily overalls.

Overalls were about the only thing he ever seemed to wear. They looked buff with a few buttons undone and his ripped pecks showing, but maybe Geraldine was getting tired of never seeing him in clean clothes, let alone stylish ones.

And he hadn't taken her out for ages. That was another thing. It was months since they'd been out to even the local restaurant. Geraldine said she didn't mind. She worked such long hours there never seemed to be an opportunity to go out on a date. Never-the-less, if he were a real man he would have insisted. He would have told her that Helga could go to hell, and forced Geraldine to take some time off so they could go out somewhere special for the night.

Or even for a few nights. That was another thing. They hadn't had a holiday together for over two years. Women like to see a bit of the world, go on romantic cruises and skiing holidays, things like that.

That was it. His mind was made up.

He'd sell the Harley. The Harley was reconditioned and ready to go. He'd fancied keeping it for himself— the cliff road on a souped up Harley was one of his dreams— but he could get good money for it, and take Geraldine on a cruise, or even to Paris. Geraldine sometimes moaned about how Helga went to Europe, and the Bahamas, Milan and Hong Cong, while she was working her fingers to the bone in Clifton to support Helga's luxury lifestyle.

Greg had never had much money. He realized now how unambitious he'd always been. He was a skilled mechanic. He could earn good wages down at the garage, or even working for a racing team, but he'd always preferred to just bumble along here at Seaside Antiques and Curios and the Seaside Guest House so he could be near Geraldine.

Yes. His mind was made up. He'd sell the Harley straight away and book a holiday for the two of them. Maybe Barbados.

He decided to find Geraldine, right now, straight away, and tell her his plans and the resolutions he'd made.

But where the hell was she?

He went hunting for her round the premises, his heart beating.

She wasn't in the shop.

She wasn't in the guest house.

This was very unusual for Geraldine at four o'clock in the afternoon.

He tried her room. She was never in her room during the day.

He knocked on the door.

"Who is it?"

Her voice sounded strange, even a bit distant.

"It's me. Greg."

"Oh. Greg. One moment."

He waited.

The moment went on and on, but still the door didn't open. What on earth was going on?

Then he heard music. A slow, thudding beat from inside her bedroom, a New Orleans beat with guitars and piano. Geraldine usually listened to classical music.

He knocked again.

"Just a minute!"

She sounded impatient. He wondered if she was impatient with him.

At long last the door opened.

The room was in semi darkness. She'd switched on a few lamps and draped some scarves over the lamps, tinging the darkness with pink shadow.

"How's my man doing?"

He was doing fine.

She was wearing a red silk chemise. Her fine, firm nipples stood up peaked and engorged beneath the lustrous material. Her cleavage glistened in the lamplight.

The chemise barely covered her butt. The flounces at the bottom lifted above her split, revealed the glistening black hairs of her bush as she raised her arms above her head, swaying in time to the music party-style. She wasn't even wearing a thong, let alone panties.

He wondered if she was drunk. He could smell alcohol. Something was driving her crazy. He ought to be worried but she was too beautiful, his cock was aching too hard to care.

CHAPTER SEVEN

GREG

He forgot about his plans and resolutions.

The chemise was bewitching. It showed off every inch of her voluptuous body. It showed off all her curves and the luscious hollows of her thighs.

"You wanta fuck me, Greg?"

She'd never spoken to him like this before. She could flirt and do intimate things, but she never talked like a whore.

She had the sort of scooped, toned breasts that were begging to be licked. She grinned—she was definitely drunk—and drizzled saliva onto a luscious curve, swooped with her head and tongued dark moisture into peaked silk. She could read his mind.

"We never have no fun, do we? All this working and worrying."

Fun?

She swayed towards him—stiletto heels in her homely bedroom?— and draped her arms round his neck. Moist lips battened on his and they kissed long and hard. Her tongue tasted burning sharp. Her breath smelled of whiskey. Geraldine was only a social drinker. She never usually got plastered like this, not at four o'clock in the afternoon.

Something was upsetting her, but as long as her pussy grazed against his throbbing cock, worrying about it wasn't possible.

He cupped her breasts in both hands. He massaged wet silk into succulent softness.

"I love you, Greg."

He didn't have time to answer. She stuffed her tongue down his throat. Her lips plastered sumptuous promises on his lips. Hot mouth meat grappled with his tongue. When he came up for air, he said:

"I love you too, Geraldine."

She kissed his ear.

"You n me are the best ever, ey Greg...?"

"I guess so."

"You wanta *take* me?"

"If you want, baby."

Take? It wasn't a word she ever used. He knew her lexicon of love from A to Z, and 'take' had never been in it. There was something cold and demanding about the word. Sex had always been alright before. Their love-making had never been anything other than perfect. And now she wanted more?

She was unclipping his overalls. Not feverishly and in haste, like yesterday, but slowly, in time to the music, kissing his chest and stomach as the bib slid down, tonguing his navel as she unfastened him at the hip, slipping down his body. Even on her knees she still swayed in time to the music as she pulled his shorts aside.

He nearly came in her mouth as her lips closed round his pulsing need of her.

His fingers ran through lustrous auburn hair, gripped two silky handfuls and held her rigid, held twining tongue and gagging wind-pipe immobile. He couldn't breathe. He was going to come. She was too much for him.

Her mouth sank slowly down his aching shaft, her lips stretching to take him all in choking herself on him, her breath heavy with whiskey and desperation, enveloping his manhood.

He tried to hold her still but slowly her mouth closed round his gathering explosion, licking and gobbling. Gagging, clucking noises blocked her throat. It was like being swallowed by a soft, sopping seashell.

He held on. There was something frantic about her. She wanted something more.

He reached the point of no return and she lifted her mouth from its feast. She knew him. She knew his body to its furthest pore, its last split second.

She sashayed over to the bed, climbed onto the rumpled mattress and knelt on her hands and knees her ass turned towards him. She spread her legs and cocked her butt.

"Take me, Greg. I'm all yours."

Take me. Take me.

Her bush glistened in the lamplight. She was sopping wet, her bush a cat's-cradle of glistening threads, creamy streaks of in her black tangle. She'd never been as urgent as this before, even yesterday.

"Wanta eat me out?"

He kicked off his overalls and took off his shoes and lay on his back and slid his mouth beneath where her sumptuous gash hovered in the lamplight.

She reached round with her fingers and pulled her lips apart. Geraldine never usually exhibited herself like this.

Her cunt was the most beautiful thing he'd ever seen, a wet orchid opening in a deranged jungle.

He lapped her moist envelope and slit it open with the tip of his tongue. She shivered. Her butt jerked. Her hot slit quaked. Her pussy banged him in the mouth. He reached around, sank yearning fingertips into her exquisite butt and held her still on his mouth.

"... Oh... oh..."

He slid his tongue up parting wetness licking for her clit, but her finger was there before him rubbing like crazy.

"... Oh... oh... oh God...!"

A hot gasket, lips, teeth, tongue, wind-pipe plunged up and down on his pounding piston. It was unbearable. 'More' was impossible. He loved her. He needed to let go. Except...

... *Take me... take me... take me...* the word wouldn't let go of him.

"... Yes... yes...!"

She was cumming in his mouth, cumming and still not satisfied.

Greg fought his way out from underneath her, a sharp taste in his mouth, his nose and chin and cheeks all wet. And she was still on all fours, kneeling on her hands and knees, her butt cocked, insisting on that obscene display.

"... Fuck me, Greg... I want you to take me... please fuck me hard..."

His throbbing tip found yearning wetness. He didn't want to fuck her hard. He needed to take his time, be loving and gentle, give her hours of pleasure, days of happiness, a whole lifetime of loving ecstasy.

The yearning wetness bucked and jerked, reared backwards and she was impaled so hard and deep on his throbbing cock he was ramming it into her like a stallion in rut.

"... Yes... yes... oh God... yes... ye-eeeeeeeeeeeeeeeeeeeeees...!"

It wasn't enough.

"... Take me... take me... I want you to take me..."

Something snapped inside him.

He flipped her over onto her back. Her feet flapped helplessly above his shoulders. He forced her knees back beneath her armpits and exposed her beautifully rounded rump. It was slippery with juice and perspiration. He was strong. His hands were powerful. When it came to spanners and engines he knew how to use force.

"... Oh... oh... ye—"

Her breath caught in her throat as he impaled her. If she wanted it rough, he'd give it to her rough.

Her butt lifted. He impaled her again and again. If she wanted brutality, he had brutality in him.

"... Yes... yes..."

She writhed beneath each savage thrust. He wasn't on the verge of climax any more. He wanted to take her, make her his, body and soul. A climax was a million miles away.

Her fingernails raked his back. She bit his chest, his throat, his ear. He'd never seen her like this before. A wild creature thrashed in his arms.

A weird sensation possessed him. A strange feeling took hold of him— as if he were someone else... as if he were another man.... No longer himself, Greg, the mechanic... a different lover entirely.

"... Oh God... yes... ye-eeeeeees..."

Her back arched as if she'd been shot. Her belly undulated against him like the swell of a hot ocean as he unleashed his aching load inside her.

"... Ye-eeeeeeeeeeeeeeeeeeeeeeeeeeeeees...!"

He exploded deep inside her. He gave her everything he had. He filled her so tight and deep his loving load was streaming out of her pulsing pussy and trickling down her sumptuous ass.

He lay on top of her for a long while, feeling the waves of pleasure still rippling through her, and through him too. He weltered in a sea of ecstasy... so how come he felt so bad?

CHAPTER EIGHT

GERALDINE

Geraldine felt bad too.

She woke up hung over. Her body ached. Her pussy was raw and swollen. Greg had done what she wanted. He'd taken her. Greg was a good guy. He didn't like it rough, but he'd done what she'd told him to... but something was still wrong...

It was Richard Braughton. That was what the problem was. She couldn't stop thinking about him. Richard's dark, brown eyes, and the willowy steel of his body inside his expensive suit, wouldn't let go of her mind.

It had happened again! Worse than just some unknown brown eyes assessing her as she fucked Greg in the car.

Last night she'd pictured all of Richard. She'd seen him, touched him, kissed him, fucked him, while she thrashed in Greg's arms. In her imagination, Richard had taken her more whole-heartedly and brutally than Greg could ever dream of.

She couldn't work it out.

No man could have given her more pleasure than Greg had given her last night. A half a bottle of Jack Daniels and her red chemise had done the trick. She'd taken it to the limit with Greg. He'd shown her her limit and he'd taken her there, and beyond... and yet all she could think about was Richard...

She couldn't possibly be in love with Richard Braughton. It was impossible. Besides from his expensive suit and his disturbingly fit body, he was the most unlikable man she'd ever met. Arrogant and pretentious. Vain and impertinent. He was one of those men who like to play mind games with women, one moment cold and harsh, the next moment tender and intimate.

He might be rich, and wear expensive clothes, but as a person, he was nowhere near as nice as Greg. And that was before she even got to the whiff of danger he gave off.

There was only one thing for it— she'd have to ignore him. She'd do her best to keep away from him.

He'd booked his room for a week. It was a long time, but if their paths crossed, she'd be businesslike and just blank him. He'd as good as said outright that he wanted to sleep with her— after five minutes, just booking into a room!— she'd make sure he'd get the message loud and clear that she belonged to another man. Someone better than him. She was already taken.

Taken. She blushed to the roots of her hair. *Taken*. It was his word. It did something to her.

Another day came round. Geraldine decided to keep busy. Keeping busy— it was the only answer.

She checked how the breakfast was going in the guest house kitchen, then opened the shop on the stroke of nine.

God knows, she had plenty of work on her plate.

Last months' receipts to go through. A cake to be ordered for the children's birthday party in room two.

Doing something about Beth and Kirsty. Kirsty just needed a good talking to. Beth was more of a problem. If Beth didn't pull her socks up quick smart she'd have to sack her, and Geraldine hated sacking people.

She had plenty to do... *and Mrs Daley's jewelry to price up!*... she still hadn't had a chance to look at Mrs Daley's stuff.

Geraldine opened the safe and took out the carrier bag full of jewelry the old lady had given her.

She sighed. Mrs Daley's jewelry was so out of date and tatty, it was hardly worth the trouble of going through it. The profit on these old jet brooches and Wedgwood cameos was so small they didn't deserve the space they'd take up in the window. The two hundred dollars she'd given Mrs Daley was far more than the whole load of junk was worth.

She ought to just take the whole lot back to Mrs Daley as unwanted, and let her keep the two hundred dollars. The old woman obviously valued her trinkets, even if no one else did. These worthless pieces were clearly precious to her. They probably carried memories of long ago happiness and long lost dreams of love.

Geraldine spread the pieces of jewelry out on the counter and started going through them.

The shop bell rang. She looked up, startled.

It was Greg!

Greg usually came in through the back entrance, from the garages, when he dropped in on her in the shop. But today he walked into the shop through the front door, straight off the sidewalk outside!

Her eyes opened even wider.

He was wearing a suit!

Geraldine couldn't remember the last time she'd seen Greg in a suit. It was his blue suit he'd worn when he first met her. The suit was old and not very expensive, but blue suited Greg's blonde hair and blue eyes and powerful physique. He looked great.

Her mouth dropped open.

He was carrying a bunch of flowers! She and Greg were long past the flowers and chocolates stage.

Greg thrust the flowers into her hand.

"... For... for... yesterday..."

"Yeah..." She didn't know what to say. "... Yesterday was great..."

A drunken fuck at four o'clock in the afternoon. It *had* been wonderful. She didn't know why she felt so awkward.

Greg blushed.

"... There'll be plenty more yesterdays..."

She had a horrible feeling that he'd prepared himself to say something to her. Something deep and personal.

"...I certainly hope so..." Her voice came out high and brittle. "...You're wonderful, Greg..."

She leaned across the counter and kissed him. She held his mouth with hers, and flirted with her tongue until his lips parted and their tongues were grappling, raking up memories of yesterday.

"... Yeah, well... I hope I'm gonna be wonderful for the rest of our lives together, Geraldine..."

God! He was going to propose! Again! Only this time it felt different. She pressed her mouth to his and searched for his tongue again.

The doorbell jangled.

She felt Richard's dark brown eyes upon her before she even fully registered who had just walked in. It wasn't even his expensive cologne or the stylish sheen of his merino/silk weave. She sensed Richard's presence in the shop as if it was a thrill of danger that had just pushed open the door.

She drew her mouth back from where she'd been leaning across the counter to kiss Greg. Her face burned.

Oh well. At least this demanding man would know now that she had a boyfriend. He'd see that she was committed to Greg. She wouldn't have to plead or make excuses or explain anything if he tried to hit on her.

"... R... Richard... Mister Braughton... Can I help you...?"

He arched an eyebrow at the pair of them, her and Greg. Even with a sneer on his face he was breathtakingly handsome.

"It doesn't look like it."

Greg stiffened. Greg instantly bristled. His fingers twitched like his fist was about to clench.

Richard smiled. He enjoyed seeing Greg angry. Greg was tough. He was good with his fists, but there was something in Richard Braughton that said he wasn't afraid of anyone.

He beamed at her:

"Well, actually. I'm looking for a present. I need a gift... for someone special."

Her. He meant her. He made sure Greg would see that she was 'someone special.'

He stretched out his hand to Greg.

"Braughton. Richard Braughton. And you are...?"

"Greg. Greg Smith."

Greg wanted to hit him. That much was clear. Greg immediately wanted to punch this presumptuous, maddeningly handsome man, but good manners got the better of him, and they shook.

She could see Greg trying to crush some discomfort into the handshake, but Richard's handshake, though somehow cool and suave, was as powerful as Greg's mechanic's grip.

Geraldine smiled.

"What did you have in mind, for the lucky person?"

Richard stroked his chin and smiled. She prayed that Greg couldn't feel what Richard's smile was doing to her.

"Mm. Well. It's got to be something special..." He cast his eye over a display of Victorian rings. "... She's a very special lady... money's no object..."

He'd instantly sussed Greg's cheap suit and cut-price shoes.

Greg sucked in a deep breath. Richard was trying to wind him up and Greg was taking the bait.

"I'm afraid most of our stuff's on the cheap side," said Geraldine.

Richard frowned at a rack of necklaces.

"Mm. I can see that."

He was quite insufferable. But his impertinence only made her heart race faster. He'd already awoken a slick of desire between her legs. She murmured:

"We do have a few nice things though."

"You think so?" Richard cast a connoisseur's eye over the shop in general. "She's not someone you can give seaside tat too."

He was outrageous. Geraldine's heart only beat the faster. This man only gave a woman the best. The best jewelry. The best clothes. The best love making. She said:

"That's a bit harsh."

She felt she ought to stick up for Helga's stock.

His eyes brightened.

"What?! Wait a second! Let me see!... this might do... this might do very well indeed...!"

He picked up a diamanté and emerald butterfly brooch from Mrs Daley's trinkets spread out on the counter.

"Yes! Very nice! Very nice indeed." He held the butterfly brooch up to the light "Mm-mmm. Obviously genuine..."

Geraldine couldn't help laughing. She was a little bit disappointed in him. He talked like a connoisseur, but he didn't know fake diamonds and glass emeralds when they were staring him in the face

".... Yes. Fabergé... genuine Fabergé..."

Geraldine wondered if she should set him straight. Richard produced a wallet:

"... I'll take it... Fabergé... it'll suit my friend perfectly... how much is it...?"

Geraldine felt even more flustered. Fabergé? He clearly didn't know a thing about antique jewelry.

She hadn't had a chance to price the butterfly brooch. She hadn't even looked at it closely yet. Ten dollars? Twenty? Fifty, at the very most?

"... Erm..."

Her loyalty to Helga kicked in. If he thought the brooch was genuine she could charge him a hundred and make a good profit for the shop. Two hundred. More. If he was deluded enough to think the brooch was genuine Fabergé she could ask anything she liked and recoup the money she'd paid Mrs Daley.

No. No way. Tricking him felt wrong. Taking advantage of his foolishness—trying to impress her in front of Greg—would be unforgivable. Two hundred. Two hundred dollars was just right. She'd make back the money she'd given Mrs Daley for her worthless jewelry and they'd all be even. She said:

"I'm afraid that one's two hundred dollars, sir."

His mouth dropped open. It was his turn to look bamboozled. His surprise seemed genuine.

"Only two hundred?!" His suavity reasserted itself in an instant. *"Is that all?"*

He smiled at her as if she was an idiot.

"Yes." Geraldine bristled. "Two hundred dollars!"

He shrugged.

"I'll take it!"

As he handed the butterfly back to Geraldine to be wrapped, a big hand closed over the brooch.

"Sorry, mate," said Greg. "It's not for sale."

Richard frowned.

"What do you mean 'not for sale'?"

"You heard me." Greg could be terribly rude too sometimes. "Not for sale. Unavailable. It's already been sold." He grinned at Richard. "To me!"

Geraldine's face burned. Greg had seen that Richard wanted to buy the brooch for her and it had pushed him into doing something stupid.

"To you?" said Richard.

"Yes," said Greg. "I just came in to pay for it."

Richard had his wallet out. There were two crisp hundred dollar bills in his hand.

Greg reached in his pocket and pulled out a roll of cash. He counted off ten twenties.

Geraldine stood between the two men, her face scarlet. She didn't know what to say. She had no idea what to do. Both of them were thrusting money at her.

"I told Geraldine I'd take it earlier," said Greg. He'd told her no such thing!

Richard looked at her accusingly.

"You said it was for sale." She hadn't said that either.

She wavered.

"... Yes... look... no... I'm afraid... yes... *Greg's right!...*"

She took the mess of twenty dollar notes clutched tightly in Greg's hand.

"...I'm ever so sorry Richard..."

She thrust the money in the till and quickly wrapped the brooch in tissue paper.

"... I remember now... yes... Greg said this morning that he wanted it..."

Richard shrugged.

His frown vanished. He was angry, but his self control was absolute. In the flash of an eye missing out on the butterfly was water off a duck's back.

He turned to go. He looked straight at Geraldine and said:

"No problem."

RICHARD

Outside, in the street, Richard's frown returned. So. She had a boyfriend. That oaf in the cheap suit.

Richard's frown slowly morphed into a smile. Her already having a boyfriend only made him want her the more. The fact that she was Greg's only made his firm intention even firmer. He was going to take her.

It was a pity about the brooch, though. Those diamonds were definitely genuine, and it was Helga's birthday next week.

CHAPTER NINE

GERALDINE

Geraldine felt relieved, but also a little disappointed. She was out of danger. At least Richard knew now that she had a boyfriend, and he wouldn't bother her any more, but at the same time she couldn't help feeling a little low. It had been nice dreaming about Richard, about getting to know him better, even if it had only been a fantasy.

But that was it. That little daydream was over now and Richard had hardly left the shop and Greg was pressing her to have dinner with him this evening at Severiano's. Severiano's! The best restaurant in Clifton.

"I've booked a table. I'll pick you up at seven."

She knew what was coming. He'd present her with the butterfly brooch— all nicely wrapped up— over dinner. She had a suspicion Greg had even more than the brooch on his mind. She had a strong feeling that he was going to propose to her again, propose more insistently than he'd ever proposed before... and she wasn't sure what she'd say.

For years Geraldine had assumed that one day she and Greg would get married, but she'd never really encouraged him. She certainly hadn't ever done anything to push him into taking the step of proposing. She loved him, but his lack of ambition and permanent pair of overalls had made her quite happy to just rub along together as boyfriend and girlfriend.

Sex with Greg was okay, she'd never asked for more, but now a part of her hankered after something more dangerous, even for the glamorous city life where danger lurked. A side of her she never even knew she had until a few days ago longed to rub shoulders with celebrities and meet dashing men like Richard Braughton. She'd always stifled feelings of ambition but she realized now that part of her really wanted wealth and power and adventure like her boss, Helga, had.

She'd worked her fingers to the bone to finance Helga's New York lifestyle. It wasn't fair.

Oh well. Those dreams were over now. Awoken and abandoned in the space of a few days. And here was Greg in his one and only suit asking her to have dinner with him at Severiano's. She said:

"I'm sorry, Greg. I've just remembered." She wasn't putting him off. She had just remembered too. "I promised the Stapletons that I'd have dinner with them this evening."

It wasn't a lie. Greg looked disappointed, but in fact she was telling the truth. The Stapletons were regular customers at the guest house, a middle aged couple who came every summer and always took Geraldine out to dinner—at Severiano's— on the last night of their stay. Tonight. It wasn't her favorite night out, but Helga liked her to socialize with the regular guests as a way to hold onto them.

"Maybe tomorrow night." She kissed him on the forehead. "We can give my red chemise another try."

Greg brightened up immediately.

The day sped by. She was due to meet up with Mister and Mrs Stapleton in the restaurant at seven.

Technically, if she was entertaining guests, she ought really to keep her Gilded Age gown on. When it came to humiliating her staff, Helga was a stickler for detail.

Geraldine showered and washed her hair.

She'd rather have gone to dinner with Greg, than with the Stapletons, but at least she'd have tonight to think things over.

It was a one hundred percent certainty that tomorrow night when he took her to Severiano's Greg was going to propose.

She'd already decided that she'd say yes. She loved him, she wanted to be his wife and have a family with him, but at least tonight she'd have a chance to fully make up her mind.

She dabbed some perfume behind her ears and did her face with extra care.

She looked at her Gilded Age gown in the mirror and shuddered. No. Bugger it. She refused to go to Clifton's premier restaurant looking like 'la belle dame sans merci.' She pulled the ghastly thing off over her head.

She chose a red, sequined, knee-length evening dress. She hadn't worn it for a long while, but the dress still fitted perfectly.

The plunging neckline showed off her cleavage to advantage. The skirt was long, but slit up one side almost to her hip, so that it showed off her long shapely legs. The red sequins clung to her belly so tightly it felt as if she'd slipped into a spangled snakeskin.

She spun around in the mirror. The dress was completely wrong. It was far too sexy for the Stapletons. Mister and Mister Stapleton were in their sixties, they'd be sure to disapprove of so much cleavage, but she didn't take it off.

Geraldine had a mournful feeling that tonight was her last night of freedom, and she wanted to look good.

Heads turned as she walked into the candlelit ambience of Severiano's. The murmur of polite conversation paused for a moment.

The Stapletons were sitting at a table in the center of the room, waiting for her.

Mister Stapleton rose to his feet as she approached. He hurried round and drew back a chair for her. He had chivalrous old-fashioned manners.

"You're looking lovely tonight, Geraldine," said Mrs Stapleton.

"Simply stunning!" said her husband.

They were a nice old couple. Geraldine had grown fond of them over the years.

"Shall we order?" said Mister Stapleton.

He picked up the large menu. The menu looked a bit like a leather-bound artist's portfolio. Severiano's was nothing compared to the restaurants in New York where Helga ate, but it still stirred a longing in Geraldine's stomach.

As they perused the starters, Geraldine heard a ringtone. It was Mister Stapleton's phone. He took the phone out of his pocket and pressed it to his ear.

"... What?... oh... really?... eh?..."

He looked at his wife. Geraldine caught a twinkle in his eye.

"Our daughter! Lucy! Lucy's back at the guest house! She's come down to see us about something..." He smiled at Geraldine. "... Something urgent, I'm afraid... she's only got an hour then she's got to get back to..."

Before Geraldine knew what was happening, the Stapletons were on their feet, apologizing profusely.

"I'm dreadfully sorry, Geraldine."

"I'm so so sorry we've got to leave you..."

"Do stay!"

"Yes! Please! Stay! Eat! Drink! Be merry!"

They were a crazy old couple.

"... Please stay... eat!... drink!... we'll cover the bill..."

Geraldine didn't know what to say. Mister and Mrs Stapleton were already on their feet.

She didn't know what to do. The Stapletons were already hurrying towards the door, looking terribly pleased and embarrassed and... a man... a man in a merino/silk suit... was rising from a table in the corner... he walking towards where she sat...

Richard sat down.

"May I join you?"

His smile did something to her stomach.

"I..."

His dark brown eyes drank her up.

He snapped his fingers and a waiter appeared.

"Shall we order?"

"How...?"

A waiter was already pouring wine into her glass.

He raised his glass.

"To us!"

"Us?"

He hand closed over hers on the tablecloth.

"Yes. Us."

His eyes, that had seemed so harsh and cold, were suddenly warm and soft.

"I want you, Geraldine."

"Yes, but..."

"And when I want something, I always get it."

His impertinence was breathtaking. He was monstrous. He'd approached the Stapletons behind her back. How he could have learned of her rendezvous with the old couple was beyond her. He'd had the gall to propose that they embarrass themselves in this ridiculous way for his sake. How had he even pulled it off? Money? Charm? Some bizarre about love? Her heart thundered in her chest.

She lifted her glass. She breathed:

"To us!"

CHAPTER TEN

GREG

Driving back to his house from the garage, Greg passed Severiano's.

His heart sang. He was happy. Tomorrow night he was taking Geraldine to dinner! He'd give her the butterfly brooch and tell her that he loved her. She already knew but he'd make her see how much. He'd tell her that he wanted her to be his wife. So much happiness was almost too overpowering to contain in one body.

He'd been crazy drifting along all these years, and never thinking of popping the question. He must have been mad. Geraldine was the only thing he'd ever wanted in his whole life. He should have married her years ago. He knew that that was what she wanted too, to have his children and live together as husband and wife.

Now that he knew what he really wanted, having to wait a whole twenty four hours was unbearable.

God damn the Stapletons. They were sitting in there now with Geraldine, in the romantically lit restaurant, when it should have been him who was wining and dining her. He wanted her tonight.

A crazy impulse told him to park opposite the restaurant. No. The impulse wasn't crazy at all. *He could book the table for tomorrow night!* It would be better to book in person. He could make sure he got the best table-for-two in the house.

He strode across the street, whistling and jingling his car keys. He glanced through the large plate glass window.

Geraldine was sitting at a table alone with Richard Braughton! Their heads were inclined towards one another. Richard's hand lay on top of Geraldine's hand.

She'd lied to him! She wasn't having dinner with the Stapletons at all. Her dinner date with the Stapletons had only been a story to put him off!

The table was in the center of the room. He could see her clearly, Richard's hand closed around her hand on the linen tablecloth. Her lips were even bending slowly towards Richard's lips. Her eyes were gazing into Richard's dark brown eyes!

The cliff car park overlooked the beach. It was a hundred foot drop from the metal railing down to the sand below. Greg pulled up with his nose in to the railing.

For an instant he wanted to gun the engine, crash straight through the chain-link.

The bitch.

She'd betrayed him. She lied to him so she could be alone with Richard. The dress she had on made it pretty clear what she wanted from Richard.

Voices came up from the beach. It had got dark. The ocean stretched away into starry blackness. It was late, but voices were coming up the steps from the beach, chattering and laughing raucously.

Greg remembered the weird sensation he'd had last night, making love to Geraldine, how he'd felt as if he wasn't himself any more, as if he were someone else in her arms, and someone else in her heart, and someone else even in her melting pussy. The weird sensation that he'd only been standing in for another man. Richard. He'd been standing in for Richard. All these years he'd been a poor second best, till she could get her hands on the real thing.

A group of girls appeared in the pool of lamplight at the top of the stairs. Five or six of the town's wild girls, in bikinis and beach wraps. Clifton's rude girls. They didn't wear their bikinis to swim. They went topless down there, and got off with guys on the rocks behind the pavilion.

The one in the green wrap and skimpy bikini top was Beth.

The minute she saw the VW she broke away from the group and came walking over.

She opened the passenger door. It wasn't locked. She didn't ask permission. She bent her head and looked in.

"What you doin' here?"

"Nothing."

She looked away, out across the ocean.

"Where you goin'?"

"Nowhere."

She grinned.

"Can I come?"

She slid into the passenger seat and closed the door.

Her wrap fell open as he leaned across and kissed her and slid his hand between her legs.

Her mouth was hot and hungry. Her tongue tasted of spearmint. She drew her head back a second and took a piece of chewing gum out of her mouth and threw it on the floor. Her mouth returned to his even hungrier.

He could feel the heat between her legs before he even touched it. His fingertips slid under her bikini bottom, and there it was, a burning wetness. Her pussy bucked the instant his fingers slipped inside.

They were just kissing, his big powerful mouth battening on her succulent little cupids-bow.

He didn't want to fuck her. He had no intention of making love to her. He only wanted to feel her heat, how it throbbed for him and moistened to his touch. He just needed to feel wanted, even if it was only by the snaky body of a girl he didn't like.

"Fuck, Greg... what's come over you...?"

"Nothing... nothing's come over me..."

"Feelin' lonely, or somethin'?"

There was a jeering edge to her voice. All the years he'd rejected her had hurt her pride.

"Geraldine got the rags on, or somethin'?"

It hurt him to hear Geraldine's name spoken in that poisonous tone, but his cock was getting stiff, and her pussy was getting slippery, rising and falling, riding his hand.

He reached across her body and pulled the lever that dropped the seat. The upholstery collapsed and she was lying flat on her back with her legs twining round him, dragging him down.

"Wow!"

Her breasts were small and taut beneath the flimsy triangles of her bikini top. His mouth closed over a toned little mound, triangle and all. He pinned between with his teeth and licked hard. Her nipple stood up like a miniature flagpole, quivering with desire.

"... Oh... oh... oh..."

He'd always thought that desire was something voluptuous and generous, like Geraldine's desire, he'd never realized that a tough, snaky little body like Beth's could be so passionate.

A hot swamp quaked in his palm. He didn't know how many fingers he had inside her the wet spasms nibbled so hard at his knuckles.

"... Oh God... yes... ye-eeeeeeees..."

She was climaxing. She was cumming already, riding his hand.

He wondered if all these mean little hard-nuts like Beth always came this quick. It certainly wasn't him she was going over the brink for. She was jerking and bucking in triumph at getting one over on Geraldine. He didn't mind. Good luck to her. Greg didn't mind at all.

"... Yes... ye-eeeeeeeeeeeeeeeeeeeeeeeeeeeeees...!"

Her climax was wild and wet, slithering under his fingers.

At least he didn't have to feel guilty about not making love to her now. She'd had her orgasm, he didn't need to go any further.

She unzipped his flies and reached inside and dragged his cock out of his shorts.

She whistled!

"Fuck, Greg! I knew you was big, but this is somethin' else!"

In spite of himself, he felt a flutter of soothed pride. Her fingernails traced the ridge of his glans. A hot palm closed round his shaft. It pumped expertly. Nineteen years old, and she was probably more experienced than he was. She grinned.

"Lucky Geraldine!"

She was disgusting.

He kicked his pants off and lay down along the seat beside. There wasn't enough room. His swollen tip traced slippery pictures up and down her hip. What had happened to that freaking bikini?

He lifted off the seat—she was light as a feather—and slid underneath her.

She went to straddle him.

"My face! Sit on my face!"

He didn't want to make love to her. He just wanted to feel needed.

Her pussy landed on his face. He felt needed alright. A swamp of hot desire enveloped chin, cheeks mouth, jerking backwards and forwards, yearning for his tongue. His tongue-tip found her voracious wetness dead center. A shiver ran up her spine. She planted both her hands on his hips and ground her quaking quagmire down harder on his mouth.

"... Fuck, Greg... shit, man..."

She was alright. Beth was tough and nasty, she was sexually precocious, but she was generous too, in her own way. She might well be a screwed up teenager, but when she gave herself she gave herself utterly. Even just a stray fuck in a car, she held nothing back. She was great.

He gave his tongue to her with all his heart. He licked and probed her sopping lips. He clamped her clit on the verge of biting and plastered her nub with loving spittle. She was lovely. Beth was beautiful in her own way.

Her mouth had already found his cock. Her lips were hot and wet. She took him in deep. She was as generous with her mouth as she was with her pussy.

His body begin to rock and lift as her tongue found depths and crannies of desire he never knew he even had in him.

She drew her mouth away and his heart caught in his throat. Her melting gash lifted from his mouth and he groaned out loud.

"... Fuck me, Greg... please... I love..."

She was too young. She didn't know what love was.

The upholstery squeaked. She spun lightly on one knee. He wasn't fucking her, her pussy was just straddling his dick, hovering, fluttering above his pounding need, voluptuous wetness twitching on his aching tip, impaling itself, a bony heat slamming itself down hard where the ache was worst, bucking and kicking and riding him hard before she even hit rock bottom.

"... Yes... yes..."

She was too light and lightly-built to grind such lavish need into the place of pain. She jerked too fast. Her tail-bone bucked too helplessly. Her hips flowed through his hands like molten wings.

"... Shit I love you, Greg..."

She didn't mean it. She couldn't mean it. She mustn't mean it. Meaning it only made things worse.

"... Oh fuck, man... you're wicked...!"

Wicked was more like it. Except their bodies were moving in sync. The waves of ecstasy and desire flowing through him were flowing through her too. Her thin, snaky body poured over him like molten lava over a burning tree trunk.

"... Fuck me, Greg... please... fuck me... fuck me hard..."

The jolt lifted him off the seat, her scrawny body flailing on his dick, her orgasm the most beautiful thing he'd ever felt in his life.

"... Yes... yes... oh God... yes... ye-eeeeeeeeeeeeeeeeeeeeeeeeeeeeees...!"

Wave after wave of ecstasy surged up his dick and went off deep inside her. Pile-driver after pile-driver juggled her sweet butt in the air unloading helpless ecstasy again and again into her sopping slit.

It was over. They lay panting and sticky in the darkness on the collapsed seat.

"Wow, Greg," she whispered. "That was something else, man."

She was back to being a tough little straycat.

He hugged her.

His heart suddenly felt empty.

CHAPTER ELEVEN

GERALDINE

Their glasses clinked.

"To us!"

Geraldine realized what she'd just said.

Perhaps it was Richard's charm, or maybe just his overbearingness, but she'd just said something that simply wasn't true.

Us?

There was no 'us'. Not she and Richard there wasn't. She loved Greg, not Richard. She didn't even like Richard very much. He was bossy and manipulative. He was unbelievably impertinent. Why had she just drunk 'to us'?

She felt herself blushing to the roots of her hair. *She'd seen him, touched him, kissed him while she made love to Greg.* She made herself think it: *she'd fucked him while she thrashed in Greg's arms.*

But that was just fantasy. It didn't mean anything. You're allowed to dream. Dreaming has nothing to do with what's serious and important.

She could feel him enjoying the way her face was burning.

He was making stupid small talk about her dress. She looked stunning in her Gilded Age gown—he was appallingly sarcastic—but red sequins were more *her*.

He looked her up and down.

In fact the red sequins clashed with her hair. Her hair was a dark auburn more than red, it didn't go with the slutty crimson of the frock. Why the hell had she chosen it?

He glanced at the glittery scarlet plunge of her cleavage.

"Yes. Exactly how I pictured you myself."

She sipped some wine from her glass, avoiding his eyes.

He had a way of getting what he wanted, of overpowering a woman— he no doubt did this with all his women— but that didn't mean she had to be his plaything.

She pretended to smile:

"I thought I was having dinner with the Stapletons." She resented the knowing hauteur playing round the corners of his lips. "What on earth did you do to make them get up and leave like that?"

He shrugged.

"I didn't *make* them do anything. They delivered you into my hands of their own free will!"

"Don't be ridiculous!" She frowned. She had every right to feel angry. "It was embarrassing for them. Sitting down to dinner then jumping up and leaving the minute I appeared. You made them look foolish. You're making *me* look foolish."

"You could never look foolish, my dear."

He was insufferable.

"What do you mean 'the Stapletons delivered me into your hands'? I don't like being delivered into people's hands!"

If she had any gumption she'd get up and walk out, leave *him* looking foolish.

An eyebrow lifted.

"We'll see."

A shocking realization hit her.

"I hope you didn't give them money!"

He was quite capable of using money to get his way. As if she were a chattel in a shop. The Stapletons weren't wealthy people. Perhaps they'd had their asking price.

Richard studied the wine sluicing around the bottom of his flute.

"Of course I didn't give them money. I did something far more horrible than that."

"*Ey?*"

Now was teasing her! He could pour his dark-eyed dashing lover look into her eyes till the cows came home. She wasn't about to be teased.

"I told them I loved you."

Her heart stood still in her chest.

"Don't be ridiculous!"

He shrugged. He didn't even pretend he was serious.

"It's not ridiculous. I told them that I adore you. That I've got to have you."

He squeezed her hand. A tingle of excitement ran through her body. She was betraying Greg. She loved Greg. She was betraying Greg in her thoughts but that didn't mean she had to betray him with her body.

"I do adore you, Geraldine." What a crazy word, 'adore'! "And I do intend to have you."

He smiled. Just a smile was enough to turn the tingle to a hot slick between her legs.

"The Stapletons are old, but they still remember what it's like to feel young and romantic. Yes. I gave them some cash, but it was my adoration that swung it."

It was the churned up feeling in her stomach, not the moisture between her legs, that was bending her lips across the table towards his. Their tongues found one another.

They were kissing! They were kissing in public! There were people in the restaurant who knew her!

She jerked her head away. Her face was burning.

"No!"

"Yes."

"... Look... I like you, Richard... I... I enjoy... having dinner with you..." They hadn't even ordered! "... But I'm going out with Greg. In fact..." She blurted. "... I love him!... Greg and I are going to be married..."

Greg had been on the point of proposing to her again today, in the shop before Richard came in. She and Greg had always known that one day they'd be married.

Richard shrugged.

"So? You're marrying Greg? That doesn't change anything. I still want you. I'm still going to have you."

She laughed out loud. Now he really was being ridiculous. Except... her heart was hammering like crazy..

"Don't be silly!"

Red sequins clung to her belly like a pulsing snakeskin. Slit frock breathed all the way up to her hip. Her plunging neckline was the most inappropriate thing she could have possibly chosen for having dinner with an old couple like the Stapletons. She'd worn this fuck-me frock for Richard. Hoping he'd be here.

Their dinner arrived.

"I already ordered." said Richard. "I hope you don't mind."

".. No... no... I don't mind..."

Dover sole and rollmops. Severiano's specialized in seafood.

She managed to calm down a bit.

Geraldine ate, barely tasting what she put in her mouth.

"Delicious!"

She drank some more wine.

He was a demanding, overbearing man. She sensed that he made demands on a woman, physical as well as emotional demands, that other men would never even dream of making. And yet, it was possible to relax and feel at ease with him in a way that she'd never relaxed or felt at ease with a man before. He made her feel that, even eating delicious food and drinking wine in a crowded restaurant, the two of them were alone in all the universe.

"I expect Greg bought that butterfly brooch to give to you," he said.

She didn't like the condescending way he spoke about Greg, but she didn't protest.

"Yes," she sighed. "I expect so."

His smile turned mocking again.

"I'm surprised at you, Geraldine. Running a jewelry shop and not being able to pick real diamonds."

She nearly dropped her fork.

"Real diamonds? You're joking!"

He was laughing at her.

"One hundred percent genuine. You've never heard of the Fabergé butterfly?"

Her face was burning.

"... Well... yes... but..."

She couldn't tell whether he was joking or not. His smile was suave and ironical, and yet his tone was deadly serious.

"I'm surprised you never noticed."

"... But... you saw the other tat... Mrs Daley's stuff is all the cheapest reproduction...genuine Farberge?... that's impossible..."

He shrugged.

"I'm telling you. The brooch is genuine. Early eighteen-nineties Farberge. Worth around a hundred and fifty thousand dollars, I'd say... without having looked at it closely, that is..."

"A hundred and fifty thousand dollars?"

He refilled her glass.

"You have a look. Tomorrow. When Greg gives it to you."

Geraldine felt flustered. Richard could disturb her equanimity so easily. She swigged some wine to cover her embarrassment. He really was impossible. One minute you were at your most relaxed and intimate with him, the next minute you felt like a complete laughing stock.

"... But... if the butterfly's genuine... what am I going to do..."

No. The brooch couldn't be Fabergé. He was just pulling her leg.

The longer the evening went on the more decided she became that she must stay faithful to Greg. Greg loved her. He loved her deeply, and she loved him. Her future lay with Greg. She was determined to stay loyal to him.

The man sitting opposite her, making sophisticated conversation, squeezing her hand, at moments whispering wild suggestions in her ear, was attractive. There was no doubt about it. Geraldine admitted to herself that she felt strongly drawn to him. Richard was refined, and powerful with it. But he was also dangerous. She could feel it in her bones, along with the ache of desire. Richard Braughton was ultra attractive... but no... he was a too great a risk.

Surely he wouldn't dream of pushing things further. He was too much of a gentleman to force himself on her. But if he tried he'd get a prompt refusal.

Their meal was ended.

"I'll drive you home."

He drove a brand new BMW. The Dakota leather upholstery was red, the same shade of red as her dress. The new leather smelled good.

Cruising through the quiet streets, she felt his hand on her leg, high up, where the slit exposed her thigh. He was impossible. He knew she wasn't going to sleep with him but he acted as if he'd already taken her.

She didn't push his hand away. He could do what he liked. She simply wasn't going to go to bed with him.

"I intend to have you, Geraldine."

She gave a light laugh.

"Is that so?"

He squeezed her thigh. A delicious shiver of heat went through her whole body.

"You wait and see."

'Wait' was exactly what she wanted to do. She could wait long and dreamily and voluptuously, except Greg was going to propose to her tomorrow.

He said he 'adored' her. But adoration has nothing to do with real love.

No. She was better off with Greg.

CHAPTER TWELVE

GREG

Greg woke next morning feeling wretched. The details of the night before rushed back upon him in all their lurid detail.

He'd betrayed Geraldine. He'd cheated on the woman he loved. He hadn't planned it. He hadn't set out to have sex with Beth. It had just happened. Even while they were at the foreplay stage he'd imagined he could merely titillate Beth, and himself too, without going all the way.

Even just groping a screwed-up teenager like Beth was bad enough, but it would have been better than this. Stopping at foreplay would have been some sort of faithfulness to Geraldine. But he hadn't stopped. He'd fucked Beth. He'd fucked his brains out with a girl he didn't even like. When he drove her back to her house they'd screwed again, in the car.

Seeing Geraldine in Severiano's with Richard had hurt. The fact that Geraldine had lied to him about having dinner with the Stapletons so she could go out with Richard had cut him to the quick. But Geraldine's betrayal wasn't as great as his. Dining with a man, even holding his hand and gazing into his eyes, wasn't the same as fucking the town slut in the back of a car.

There might even be some innocent explanation for why Geraldine had ended up at the restaurant with Richard instead of the Stapletons. The old couple might have canceled, and she might have just run into Richard immediately after the Stapletons had let her down, and Richard might have offered to take her to Severiano's instead. It could even have been some maneuver of Richard's. The guy was a snake.

Greg groaned. He rolled out of bed. He didn't want to get dressed. He couldn't face his old oily overalls. He couldn't face anything.

He went to the bathroom and looked in the mirror. His face was haggard. He could see what he'd done last night in every crease and hollow. Even a stranger would pick up on the marks of his night's debauchery, let alone Geraldine.

The butterfly brooch he'd bought to give to Geraldine was still in the pocket of his suit jacket.

He unwrapped the tissue paper and looked at it.

The brooch was pretty. Points of light glittered in the green and blue facets of the butterfly's wings. 'Paste' Geraldine called it, imitation diamonds.

Two hundred dollars had been a lot of money for him. He scowled at the brooch. No doubt smooth-talking Mister Richard Braughton could afford to buy Geraldine far more expensive jewelry than this.

Still. The brooch was pretty, and he'd bought it to give to her. He had to give it to her, as a token of his love, no matter how bad he felt. He'd planned to give Geraldine the brooch and propose to her at the same time. His plan had been to wrap up the brooch nicely, and give it to Geraldine and ask her to be his wife at one and the same moment.

Except... he couldn't ask her to be his wife after what he'd done last night. At least... he couldn't ask her to marry him until he'd told her that he'd slept with Beth and asked her to forgive him. He and Geraldine had always been totally honest with one another. He couldn't stop being honest now, not when it came to something as important as marriage.

Yes. The first thing he had to do was tell Geraldine about Beth. Geraldine was generous. She might forgive him, and then he could propose to her with a clear conscience.

Then again... she might not forgive him...

He showered and shaved. He slapped a load of aftershave onto his face. It would be terrible if Geraldine *smelled Beth* on his skin. He put on his suit. He always felt awkward in his suit.

He found some wrapping paper and wrapped up the brooch carefully and neatly.

He realized that he had to be strong. If he wanted to win Geraldine he had to be honest. Yes, when he gave Geraldine the butterfly, he'd confess about his night with Beth and still ask her to marry him.

He and Geraldine had had a long, committed relationship. They knew one another inside out. They loved one another. Geraldine would be shocked. Of that there could be no doubt. Geraldine would be shocked and hurt. But she had a generous heart. Geraldine was the most generous and forgiving woman you could hope to meet. Surely she'd forgive him. He knew that she would. She loved him, and, in spite of her shock and hurt, she'd still want to marry him.

At least... he had to take that risk.

Greg turned off the main road and drove down the side alley next to Helga's Seaside Antiques And Curios to the garages. His heart was in his mouth.

He parked the VW and got out.

A man in a leather jacket was standing outside the locked door of his workshop.

"Greg? How's it goin' man?"

The guy had a bushy beard and lots of earrings.

"Jimbo?"

"Yeah. That's me."

It was the guy who'd offered to buy the Harley! Greg had been so busy yesterday, and then so freaked out last night, he'd forgotten all about agreeing over the phone to sell the Harley Davison to Jimbo.

Greg opened up the workshop. He felt a reluctant foreboding gather in his stomach as he slid the shutter up.

"Wow, man! She's a beauty!"

The reconditioned Harley certainly looked good. The paintwork was crisp and shiny. The engine was in tip top working order. All at once Greg didn't want to sell it.

"Five grand?"

Jimbo was pulling a fat roll of banknotes out of his pocket!

"... Erm..."

He'd put so much love and hard work into the motorbike, surely he couldn't let somebody just ride off on it.

The five thousand dollars would take Geraldine on a holiday somewhere nice. It would help towards setting up house when they got married. If they got married.

Maybe Geraldine wouldn't want to marry him now.

He loved that Harley. Perhaps he'd be better off keeping it.

"Here you go! Five big ones!"

Jimbo was thrusting the money at him. He knew a bargain when he saw one.

'When you be finished the Harley Greg? I'm dyin' for a ride.'

A glimpse of thong under a frilly apron.. He felt ill.

He grabbed the roll of money, and shook the new owner's hand.

"She's all yours, Jimbo. Enjoy!"

CHAPTER THIRTEEN

RICHARD

Richard drove at high speed out of Clifton. He swung his BMW out onto the freeway.

He felt pissed off.

He resented having to leave Clifton at such a critical moment. It infuriated him having to run this stupid errand when his affair with Geraldine hung in the balance.

Geraldine might not call it an affair, but he did.

Last night he'd come close to getting her into bed. She'd put up some resistance— he liked women who put up some resistance— but she'd been close to succumbing. He'd felt her warming to his charm. She'd been on the point of surrendering her scruples about that oaf, Greg.

He could tell. Sitting beside him in his BMW as he'd driven her home, she'd been on the point of throwing herself into his arms. Another tête-à-tête, a few more minutes, one more kiss, and Geraldine would give herself to him, and give herself sensationally, as only that type of woman can do.

Richard her never met anyone like her. 'Wait' wasn't a word he was used to. Wait, and he might lose her, might be losing her right now running this freaking errand for Helga.

He'd begun his flirtation in a spirit of light-hearted conquest. He enjoyed a bit of cut and thrust. He liked it when a woman who played hard to get. He appreciated a girl who fought back, in the full knowledge that he'd eventually take her.

But Geraldine was different. She was special. She'd entangled his feelings in a way he wasn't prepared to even fully admit to himself. She had an allure he'd never come across before. She seemed hardly aware of how attractive she was, which only made her even more attractive.

Geraldine unsettled him. She left him troubled and perplexed. She was stunningly beautiful, of course. Her body, in the red sequined evening dress last night, was the most desirable thing he'd ever seen in his life. Yet somehow she appealed to him in a way that went beyond even beauty and sex appeal.

He'd told her he loved her. Perhaps he even meant it.

And now this damned errand to run, up to the airport and back, which meant being away from her a full twenty four hours, maybe even longer, and leaving her alone in Clifton with Greg.

Greg was an oaf. He had neither ambition nor style, but Richard could see that Geraldine's boyfriend possessed a certain appeal. He was well built. He was even good looking, in a boyish sort of way.

Geraldine was big-hearted. She was a generous person. She'd been Greg's girlfriend for a long time. Her good nature might deliver her up to Greg while he was away. It was obvious Greg was planning to propose to Geraldine. He'd snatched the butterfly brooch for himself— not even knowing what the freaking thing was worth— so he could give it to Geraldine when he asked her to be his wife.

Geraldine's generous heart might make her say yes. Five years is a long time.

Richard bit his lip. He fixed his eyes on the mile after mile of concrete and bitumen speeding him away from her.

It was infuriating. Especially as Geraldine had come so close to giving herself to him last night. She'd been moments from surrendering.

Towns and seascapes, hills and farms flashed past. He could still taste her lips, her perfume, feel how voluptuously she'd abandon herself in bed. He sensed how it might even be a turning point in his life, when he took possession of her body.

And now this damned chauffeur errand to run!

Richard parked in the airport's multi-storey carpark. It wasn't a major airport, luckily. There was only one terminal.

He found the Arrivals Gate.

He looked at his watch.

It was lucky he could take the BMW up to a hundred and forty. He was just on time.

Heads turned. People stopped and stared.

A tall, slim woman wearing sunglasses, in a black slacks suit and six inch heels walked out of the Arrivals gate.

Helga always created a stir, wherever she went. She was supermodel slim, her Nordic features strikingly photogenic under the Dolce and Gabbana sunglasses.

"Richard! Darling!"

Her voice rang out, confident and commanding, across the Arrivals Lounge.

She embraced him. Men glanced with open envy.

He took her bag.

"Car's in the multi-storey."

Helga pouted. She was used to being pampered in a way that was both irritating and maddeningly attractive.

"Bored of me already, are you darling?"

"Of course not."

"That little witch down in Clifton stolen your heart away has she?"

"Don't be ridiculous."

He knew that Helga and Geraldine didn't get on. Geraldine had every right to resent the high handed way Helga exploited her. And, for all her wealth and stylishness, Helga had always seemed somehow jealous of Geraldine.

He smiled.

"How could anyone steal my heart away when I've got the most sought after lady in New York on my arm?"

Helga scowled. The compliment didn't seem to please her.

"Three nights away, and my lover doesn't want me any more!"

Richard wondered if something had changed inside him, and Helga had picked it up. She'd sensed that he had feelings for Geraldine. Helga could be almost psychically paranoid sometimes, but... no... that couldn't be. It was just Helga's usual spoiled, demanding way of talking.

They walked towards the entrance.

"I can't be bothered driving all the way down to Clifton now, darling." It was him who was driving! Not her! "We'll go down in the morning. I've booked a room in the airport hotel."

Richard felt a stab of irritation. Worse than irritation, or even anger, a churn of dread. He needed to get back to Clifton right now, and see Geraldine, and check what had happened when Greg gave her the brooch.

It was typical of Helga to have booked the hotel room without even asking him, let alone asking whether he felt like satisfying her non-stop demands.

The airport hotel had its own entrance, across a glass walkway from the terminal.

Their room was on the top floor. Helga studied her face in the mirror as they went up in the lift. Richard saw that his face was haggard. There was a wild glint in his eyes. He wondered if Helga had noticed too.

The room was small and bare. Helga tested the mattress. The bed was big but somewhat hard.

Helga looked round imperiously at the décor.

"Somewhat Spartan... but adequate for our purposes..."

They weren't 'our' purposes, just hers.

"Perhaps we can sort things out now," he said. "Before we go down to Clifton."

"Things?"

Helga pretended a lofty disinterest in the source of her mega income.

"Business.'

Helga was thinking of selling both the shop and guest house. Helga's Seaside Antiques And Curios and Helga's Seaside Guest House, weren't bringing in the sort of money she demanded. She was planning to sell up, and invest the money in one of her other, more lucrative ventures. She'd sent Richard down to Clifton to check up on the state of both businesses, and the sort of money she could expect to get for tem.

Helga draped her arms around his neck. The skintight crotch of her slacks swayed against his flies.

"Never mind business, darling. First things first..." She nodded at her suitcase. "... The stuff's in my over-night bag."

Helga stayed on her feet while Richard undressed her. She stood as still as a statue, hands on hips, one foot up on the bed, a model posing for a magazine cover, while Richard unbuttoned her black silk blouse and released her black lace bra at the back. It was like stripping a fashion dummy of its clothes in the window of an exclusive store.

Helga shrugged her blouse and jacket off.

Usually it drove him wild the way she refused to let him kiss her throat or even lick her nipples while he stripped her.

She didn't even like him to feast on her voluptuous lips in their dark cherry gloss.

Helga liked to stay passive and inert, and completely in control. She didn't allow one hair of her close-cropped, peroxide blonde hairdo to be disturbed while she was being disrobed. Normally Helga's inanimate authority drove him crazy with desire, but today something had changed.

He stooped and removed her shoes. Helga barely lifted her foot off the floor to help him, but he refused to kneel.

She barely moved to assist him, as he unzipped her slacks and pulled them down. She betrayed no sign of either urgency or passion. Helga liked to remain separate and passive while she wielded her power over him.

Richard's fingers slid coolly under the black lace of her Parisian knickers and slipped them down over her pertly rounded buttocks. He didn't feel his usual itch to touch the immaculately shaved mons beneath the silk or even graze the tightly furled crease of her pussy with his knuckles.

Helga was as cold as ice. Usually her iciness burned him up, but today Richard felt as stony cold as she was.

She trod her knickers into the carpet. She was completely naked. Richard turned her around and put her blindfold on.

The blindfold was a narrow band of leather buckled tightly over her eyes. Helga didn't like to see the person she was having sex with.

When the blindfold was secure Richard fastened the leather cuffs around her wrists.

"Foot up!"

Usually he had to kneel to buckle the leather anklets round her ankles, but today Helga heard the impatience in his voice. She obligingly put one foot at a time up on the bed while Richard fastened the leather straps round her shapely ankles.

The cuffs and anklets were attached to lengths of chain.

When her shackles were secure, Helga lay down flat on her back on the bed. She stretched her arms out on either side above her head as far as they would go and spread her legs open as far as they would go.

"Go on. Hurry up."

Moisture glistened on the furled lips of her pussy.

Helga never usually got excited this quickly. Richard's heart grew even colder.

He yearned to run his fingers through auburn hair and gather up a loving tenderness in his arms.

He fastened the four chains to the four legs of the bed. He took his time. Helga groaned out loud as he tugged her ankles further apart.

"You can take your clothes off now, darling."

"Thanks a lot."

He unbuttoned his shirt. He unbuckled his belt and unzipped his pants.

Helga didn't like to see him naked. His cock was already hard and aching, but Helga preferred not to witness the instrument that was about to impale her. She preferred to give orders in the dark.

"Don't be like that, Richard."

By the time he'd taken off his shoes off his cock was aching so badly it hurt. Helga always did this to him. She was a control freak. So was he. Her passive power— chained to the bed, barely able to flesh a muscle of those pale, exquisite thighs— never failed to arouse the impulse to take charge, the need to subdue and ravish her, but today all he felt was a cold, piercing dislike.

"Go on, Richard. Do it."

Her body was perfect. Helga's skin was flawless. Her belly was a translucent expanse of pulsating pallor. There wasn't a single bruise or welt from the last time they'd made love. There never was. Helga drove him to the point of berserk violence. She aroused and teased him till he saw red. Then, once he was beside himself with the need to inflict pain, she insisted on gentleness.

He freed his belt from the loops of his pants. It swung above her stunning split. Cartier. Palladium finish buckle. A meter of black crocodile skin. Thirty millimeters wide, the perfect width to trace the tight moisture of her exquisitely furled pussy. A Christmas gift from Helga.

Everything went dark. God, he wanted to hurt her. Give her some belt where things hurt most.

No. Their game was crueler than that.

He ran the tip of the belt up over her navel. Her belly button wasn't beautiful. Her navel was puckered and hungry like the rest of her.

An inch of smooth alligator skin—the belt was cut from the belly of the beast where alligators slide along on patterned ooze— rode the outline of her ribs, parted the shapely tightness of he breasts.

He let the belt swing lazily, flicked at a nipple. Another nipple. Her taut nubs stood up even taller and stiffer.

"...Mm-mmm...yes... that's nice... go on, Richard..."

It was a dare. It was her way of torturing him, deliberately driving him crazy, playing with his deepest darkness, screwing up his mind. Helga understood him through and through. She knew where to find the ferocity inside him. Helga could put her finger on his need to ravish and destroy with one modest twitch of her splayed split.

He ran the belt back down her belly. Her pussy lifted in response. Tongued crocodile skin at her pulsing mound. It lifted for a stroke that would never come.

"... Yes... yes... that's nice... that's... go on, Richard..."

If he stayed with her much longer he was going to do it, go on, and go on going on till she was a howling mess of welts and bloody lesions.

He dangled the belt between her legs.

"... Yes.. yes... please... oh God..."

The belt coiled a second on rumpled sheet, a cobra about to strike. He trailed it slowly up her pussy, slithered it up her moist unfurling pussy lips. When he drew it away, as if to lash out, the crocodile skin glistened with reluctant juice.

It went on and on. This pantomime. Every time. Like a surveyor laying out interminable Dragging him closer and closer to the edge.

The chains clinked against the legs of the bed as her hips bucked.

"... Okay... you can fuck me now..."

Fucking her was always a wish Helga granted, never a plea. He was a fraction of a second away from going berserk, from really doing it, from hearing her scream for mercy, then fucking her when *he* chose, not *her*.

He was breathing hard.

"You enjoy our little game, Helga?"

It was her game, not his. He needed to get free of her. He had to get as far away from her as possible. One day she was going to go too far and his vengeance would be terrible.

"Mm. Of course I do, Richard. Every time."

He knelt between her legs, taking care that his knees didn't brush against her inner thighs. Helga could only stand a little contact at a time.

Her pussy's unfurled lips closed round the tip of his cock succulently, triumphantly. Her wetness folded around him without the faintest trace of desire.

Her back arched and forced her burning gash a fraction deeper over his throbbing stillness. He had to stay still. He wasn't allowed to move. Another aching buck lifted her butt off the bed and impaled her a fraction deeper, her voluptuous wetness squeezing him, daring him to go berserk. He didn't.

"... Yes... yes... mm-mmm... mm-mmmmmmmmm..."

She couldn't help herself. Helga never had been able to help herself. The quaking of her desire grew more urgent. The chains ground against the legs of the bed as her arms strained to wind themselves around him. Her shackles clinked and tugged as her legs tried to clamp round his unmoving buttocks.

Suddenly she was grinding at him, quicker and quicker, using him just how she liked him, a flesh and blood toy.

"... Yes... now... *now*... do it...!"

She was too proud to even ask him to fuck her. 'Do it!' was all she ever gave him. It was the moment in their game when he gave himself to her, when he delivered all of himself in fury and frustration.

This time it was going to be different.

His hands slid under quaking shoulder blades. He wrapped his arms around her in a fierce embrace. He feasted on her glossy mouth as he rammed his cock into her wetness again and again, feeling her orgasm coming, an explosion gathering inside her against her will.

"... Yes... oh Richard... yes... ye-eeeeeeeeeeeeeeeeeeeees..."

Her climax, at least, was generous. Her thighs and buttocks went slippery with juice. She drove him wild. Helga always did.

Her body kicked and thrashed in ecstasy, waiting for him to let go. Richard rammed his cock into her again and again like a man possessed. He gouged and split her like he did every time, a stallion in rut mounting a bucking equestrian statue...a surge of savage delight swarming up his rock-hard dick... and she could fuck off, Helga could go fuck herself, he refused, for once in their screwed-up relationship he didn't let go. He held it in. It wasn't difficult. He refused to climax.

He was saving that for Geraldine.

CHAPTER FOURTEEN

GERALDINE

Geraldine woke one minute before the alarm went off.

She tapped the clock so she wouldn't have to listen to the jarring jangle, and slid lightly out of bed.

She felt excited, and yet calm too. There was a happy sense of peace beneath her excitement.

She'd had a thrilling evening with Richard, but she'd made up her mind to say yes to Greg when he proposed to her today, as she knew he would.

She was pleasantly hung over from the wine she'd drunk last night with Richard. And just like the soothing buzz of the wine, the memory of her evening with Richard formed a romantic halo around her down-to-earth decision to settle down with Greg.

She'd never forget Richard for as long as she lived. He'd made a deep impression on her. She felt proud at having aroused the passion of a man as formidable as Richard. The pressure of his lips against hers, his hand on her thigh in the car, were things she'd remember for the rest of her life. She'd store them away in a cherished place in her heart while she went about raising a family and living an ordinary married life with Greg.

So. What to wear for this special day? That was the next question.

The red dress, with the sequins and the split up the side, lay on a chair. No. Far too sexy for the shop. The dress meant something special to her now, after her evening with Richard. It was way too precious to wear to work.

Helga's Gilded Age gown hung on the back of the door. Geraldine was damned if she'd wear that thing ever again. She might work for Helga and depend on Helga's shop for a livelihood, but that didn't mean that Helga owned her body and soul.

What would Greg like? That was the question.

Her new slashed jeans and her white Hugo Boss T-shirt, without a bra. Yes. It was the right outfit for her new life with Greg, and today was day one.

The shop was pleasantly quiet.

Two sunburned tourists were browsing the scrimshaw display. Kirsty had taken the day off. Geraldine didn't mind at all. It would be nice, when Greg came, to have the shop to themselves.

The tourists bought a Norwegian scrimshaw and left.

When Greg came in, the shop was felicitously empty.

Greg was wearing his suit. He thrust a bunch of flowers at her. He seemed somehow reticent, awkward. Not his usual easy going self. Well... when a man's about to put his life in your hands he has every right to be reticent...

"I got this for you..." He gave her a small package wrapped in red paper. "... I guess you already realized I bought it for you..."

It wasn't a very gracious way of saying it.

"Why? What is it?"

She knew very well what the tiny parcel contained, but when she opened it and saw the butterfly brooch, she was genuinely amazed and delighted. The faceted glass flashed and glittered almost as if it was real diamond. The silver plating gleamed like real silver, and not mere gilt.

She kissed him.

"Why! Thank you, Greg. It's beautiful!"

She really meant it.

She pinned the brooch on her T-shirt.

"Ouch!"

The pin nipped her breast. She should have worn a bra. The cotton got rucked up as she pushed the pin through again and fastened it in the clip. She smoothed her T-shirt flat and ample. The butterfly rode lightly, like a breathless charm on her breast. Greg mumbled:

"... I know they're not real diamonds..."

"It doesn't matter! It doesn't matter in the slightest!"

She wished he'd get on with it. His face was troubled in a way she'd seen before.

"...But, you know how much I love you, Geraldine... and... well... I..."

He was about to say it!

GREG

It was like a clock, ticking inexorably towards doomsday.

"I got this for you..."

Greg's heart hammered as he watched Geraldine pin the brooch to her T-shirt. She was so beautiful! The butterfly looked amazing, riding on the shapely swell of her breast. There wasn't a woman in the world to match Geraldine.

"... I know they're not real diamonds..."

"It doesn't matter. It doesn't matter in the slightest!"

The clock reached one second to. He had to be strong. He had to tell her. Asking for her hand in marriage was impossible without telling her everything.

"... But you know how much I love you, Geraldine..."

She smiled down at the brooch without saying anything.

"... And... I've always loved you..."

She'd forgive him. Speaking shouldn't be so difficult. He felt certain she'd forgive him. And once she'd forgiven him he could ask her to marry him.

"... From the start..."

Her face was flushed with pleasure. She was waiting for him to say it.

They'd had such a long, committed relationship. They knew one another inside out. They loved one another. Surely nothing could destroy that.

"... And... well I... there's something I need to tell you..."

Geraldine would be shocked. She'd be devastated. Geraldine would be shocked and hurt. But she had a good heart. She was generous. Geraldine was the most generous and forgiving woman imaginable. She loved him, and, in spite of her shock and hurt, he knew she'd forgive him.

"What?" She smiled. "Tell me what?"

"... Oh... oh nothing... I hope you like the brooch..."

Greg spun on his heel and bolted for the door.

CHAPTER FIFTEEN

GERALDINE

Geraldine was flummoxed. One moment Greg had looked so confident and sure of himself, the very picture of a man about to propose to a woman whom he knew would accept him, the next minute a face riven by conflict, and he wouldn't even say what was tormenting him.

She thought she knew Greg through and through, but he seemed to have turned into a different man. If she didn't know better, she would almost have said he looked guilty. But that was impossible. Greg was the most honest and open guy imaginable. If he ever did anything wrong he owned up to it immediately. He never tried to back out when he made a mistake.

Geraldine was confused. More than confused, she felt disturbed. Something bad had happened. Something bad was happening right now. Upheavals were underway, and not just in her own head, the weird mood she'd been in lately. She needed to keep busy, find something to do. Thank God there were always plenty of things to do.

Everything felt wrong. Even the butterfly brooch felt wrong, riding so lightly on her T-shirt. You don't wear old-fashioned costume jewelry, no matter how beautiful, on T-shirts. In her confusion she'd pinned it on way too low. The pin was irritating her skin. A man doesn't give a woman a sentimental old piece of paste, then turn on his heel and run!

She set to work tidying the shop— Kirsty had left it in a mess again.

A coach party had rampaged through her display of shawls and furs—she shouldn't even be selling the freaking things— and left them piled on umbrellas. She stuffed fox and ermine and faded old scarves back onto their hangers.

"Never an idle moment, eh?"

Her heart stopped beating. The next instant it was hammering in her chest.

She should have got the shop bell fixed. Richard Braughton was standing in the doorway looking at her. He grinned.

"Don't you ever take any time off?"

She tried to smile.

"I took some time off to go to Severiano's and got hijacked by a domineering man."

"Really?" His grin was more than ironical, it was blatantly sarcastic. "You don't look like the type to be domineered to me."

Not the type to be domineered? He was already domineering her with his eyes, domineering her from head to toe, domineering her knees, her hips, her belly, her breasts straining at tight cotton.

No. No he wasn't. She was going crazy. It was the brooch he was surveying, the tiny weight of faceted glass and diamant paste hammering on her breast.

"I see Greg gave you your Fabergé diamonds."

Her face flushed.

"Yes... except... don't be silly..." She glanced down at the brooch, lifting and falling. "... That's not Fabergé... those aren't real diamonds..."

He gave her a superior look.

"Of course they are. That brooch is worth at least a hundred and fifty grand. Possibly more."

She tried to laugh. It felt good being able to laugh at him.

"... A hundred and fifty thousand?!... don't be ridiculous... of course it's not worth that much!... Mrs Daley is poor as a church mouse... her stuff's all tat... she'd never have anything as expensive as... *a hundred and fifty thousand..?!*"

He took her by the elbow. He was manhandling her! He was pulling her towards the door.

"That's why we need to get you out of here before Helga finds out."

"Helga?"

He nodded at the street.

"She's up at the Clifton Arms, booking in."

"She's in Clifton?"

It was wrong, this sudden panic, *as if she was scared of Helga or something*. Helga was only her boss, her employer come to cast an eye over her business. Her business was in okay shape. There was no reason for this sudden shiver of panic.

"Let's go!"

"Go?"

He wasn't domineering at all. From the minute he's walked in there'd been something changed about him, his sarcasm edgy, his supercilious manner somehow tense.

"Let's find out how much the brooch is really worth first."

It was all madness. He seemed to seriously think that the butterfly was genuine Fabergé. If it was genuine and Helga thought she'd cornered it for herself there'd be hell to pay. Even Richard seemed nervous of the hell there'd be to play.

"... But..." She looked around. "... I can't leave the shop... not like this... Kirsty hasn't shown up... there's no one to take over..."

"Can't you just close?"

"In holiday season? With Helga here?"

Crazy thoughts scrambled through her head. He must have driven Helga here. He was Helga's partner. He was Helga's boyfriend and Helga was here and he was pulling at her arm trying to take *her* away somewhere.

"Damn Helga. What about that girl in the guest house?"

"Beth?"

Beth was always so obstreperous. She was a little madam. Her manners were appalling. Beth had no idea about business in the shop, how to speak to customers, how to negotiate prices. She made a fuss about changing linen and making beds, never mind being asked to take over the shop.

As it turned out Beth was quite gracious. She didn't kick up a fuss about taking over more responsibility than she was used to. She listened while Geraldine gave her a quick rundown of shop procedure.

"Yeah. Don't worry. No problem."

They were away.

She climbed into Richard's BMW.

He closed the door for her, still the supercilious gentleman, but a tense supercilious gentleman, his movements swift and edgy.

He climbed in and started the engine.

It was all happening too fast.

"Where are we going?"

"You don't believe me?" He laughed.. "You think I'm a complete ignoramus? I'm taking you to Rose Bay!"

"Ey?"

Rose Bay was three towns along the coast. It would take at least three hours to get there, and three hours to get back. If he was even thinking of bringing her back.

"To Blanchards in Rose Bay."

"Blanchards?"

Geraldine knew Blanchards. It was the big auction house in Rose Bay specializing in antique jewelry. It was the place you went to if you wanted to have your jewelry valued by an expert.

"You heard me."

He was making a fool of her. Dragging her away from the shop, and now this. Blanchards was a high class house. The valuers there were all top experts. They'd laugh at her, walking in with Mrs Daley's butterfly!

"Helga will be furious."

"Don't you worry about Helga. I'll sort Helga out."

They sped along the cliff road. Her heart was still beating fast. She wasn't used to men who just took over like this. Sitting beside him in the passenger seat, in this very car, she remembered how, a mere two nights ago, his hand had rested on her thigh.

She wasn't wearing her sexy, split-leg skirt now, but the warm ache in her pussy, under her jeans' slashed denim, was just the same.

They swept through Portslade.

"That's where Mrs Daley lives."

She pointed out the gloomy old house with its bay windows shuttered and the paint peeling on the windowsills and its turret for viewing the ocean fogged with sea salt.

The house had altered since she was there with Greg. A dumpster stood on the street outside. It was heaped with furniture and old appliances. Men were coming in and out of the house throwing carpets and crockery into the dumpster.

"It must have been a grand house once," said Richard.

"Well it's not now," said Geraldine, a little resentfully. "It smells…" A hot sensation creased her stomach. "… I mean, smelled."

Two hours later they were in Blanchards Auction House in Rose Bay, sitting in an elegant room with one of the country's foremost experts on Victorian jewelry. They hadn't made an appointment, but Richard's commanding manner worked as well with managers of auction houses as it did with manageresses of shops.

"We just wanted you to have a look at this piece here," said Richard.

Geraldine felt stupid with the brooch hanging awkwardly on her T-shirt. She felt dazed. She should have taken it off in the car.

Richard's knuckles brushed her nipple as he unfastened it.

The auctioneer looked at the butterfly. He turned it over and examined the gilt at the back. His eyes widened. He placed his magnifier in his eye and examined the brooch front and back. He murmured:

"Magnificent! In my whole professional life I never dreamed I'd ever see one of these."

Geraldine went hot all over.

"Is it genuine?"

"Genuine?!" said the auctioneer. "It's a Fabergé alright. It's from Fabergé's finest period!"

A triumphant smile played around Richard's lips.

"How much is it worth?"

The auctioneer considered for a moment and said:

"If I were putting it up for auction, I'd start at two hundred thousand dollars."

Richard laughed.

"Damn! I was fifty grand out!"

CHAPTER SIXTEEN

GERALDINE

When they walked out of the auction house the sun was low on the horizon. A track of gold spread out across the ocean.

There was a sinking feeling in the pit of her stomach.

"I must take it straight back to Mrs Daley. Right now. I've got to return the thing to Mrs Daley. Immediately!"

The dumpster outside the gloomy old house. Men throwing bedsteads and carpets away. The sinking feeling grew heavier and heavier.

She was still shocked by what she'd just heard. She was flabbergasted at the value of the brooch pinned to her T-shirt. Richard had insisted on re-fastening the butterfly on her T-shirt instead of finding somewhere safe to put it. He was in a weird mood.

"Immediately?"

"I feel terrible. I only gave her two hundred dollars."

She felt like a criminal.

He looked at his watch:

"It's late. It's a long drive back."

"I've got to give it back to her, Richard. Right now!"

"Tomorrow!" He said it firmly. "You can give it back to her in the morning. Tonight you're having dinner with me. And after dinner you're going to sleep with me."

"Excuse me! I don't know where you get that idea from!"

He squeezed her hand. Her fingers seemed to melt in his grasp.

"Where? From your eyes, Geraldine. From your lips. From every bit of you."

She stiffened. She pulled her hand away.

"Then every bit of me's a liar."

He shrugged.

"We'll see."

He was leading her along the footpath, but not in the direction of the car, his hand in the small of her back, guiding her along the sidewalk. He had no right to push her around in this way.

"Where are we going?"

There was a taxi stand on the other side of the street. She could make a break for it, flee his imperious impetuosity, dash across the street, jump into a taxi and tell it to take her back to Clifton,... it was a long way... it would more money than she had on her, but it was still the right thing to do...

Richard guided her towards a hotel. He was leading her up the steps of the Belvedere, the most expensive hotel in Rose Bay.

He looked at her, still domineering, still imperious in everything he did, but his eyes still tense, edgy, peeled naked of everything but her.

"Aren't you hungry?"

She was starving. She'd been excited about Greg proposing to her and forgotten to eat breakfast. She hadn't had any lunch either. The sinking sensation made even the thought of eating impossible.

"A little."

"Well then... the food here's excellent..."

The Belvedere's restaurant certainly looked expensive, its brass-framed doors wide open, a palm tree on either side, soft music from within.

Richard stopped at the reception desk. A receptionist in a purple jacket hurried over to serve him.

"Yes, sir?"

"I want a room for the night."

"... Richard... no...!"

The receptionist looked from Richard to her and back again.

"For two, sir?"

"Yes. For two."

"... Richard... please..."

There must be somewhere cheaper where she could stay by herself, get the bus back to Clifton in the morning.

"A suite, if you have one. Preferably with an ocean view."

The receptionist consulted her computer.

"There's the Maha Raja Suite, sir."

"Maha Raja? Yes, that'll do."

"... RICHARD...!"

Whatever had gone wrong with Greg this morning, it was still Greg that she loved. She'd made up her mind to accept Greg's proposal of marriage. Her decision hadn't changed just because of Greg's strange behavior or because it had been such a dreadful, chaotic day.

Richard took her arm. He led her from the reception desk into the hotel's arcade of chic shops. The hotel boutiques were still open.

"Madame's hungry..." She'd said no such thing. And she wasn't freaking 'madame'! "... But you know the Belvedere..." She didn't know the Belvedere at all! She'd never been here in her life! "... Food's first class but there's a dress code I'm afraid... He looked her up and down. He devoured her with his eyes. "... You like nice in jeans, Geraldine. I know that T-shirt's Hugo Boss... but not when we're dining at the Belvedere."

The next thing she knew she was in a changing room trying on a dress that Richard had chosen.

She hadn't even had a say in the matter!

She took her jeans off. She felt as if it was her past, the whole of her life that had gone before, that she was slipping out of. The slashed denim clung to her legs. It didn't want to let her go. It was her former life she was taking off, the butterfly bundled up in the bunched cotton, as she pulled her T-shirt over her head!

She looked at the frock hanging on the rail. What impertinence the man had!

Black! Black chiffon! She didn't feel like wearing black. Black didn't suit her. The chiffon sheer and lustrous, the skirt extra short, a bandeau bodice as if she was some hot little wannabe out to catch her a VIP.

With all his hubris and supercilious hauteur you would've thought Richard would've had more taste.

He did have more taste. His choice was unerring. Black. Shiny lustrous black. A chic mourning frock. For a funeral. Richard knew something terrible was happening too.

She put it on. The dress was extra tight and very short, the bandeau bodice sheer across her breasts and arms, as if he'd decided to bind her.

A glance in the mirror. She looked stunning.

She climbed into the five inch Jimmy Choos he'd bought her— metallic black peep-toe strappy sandals— and looked even more stunning.

She swayed out of the dressing room with her jeans and T-shirt over her arm and her trainers in her hand.

The assistant provided a carrier bag.

Richard rescued the brooch from the carrier bag and insisted on pinning it on her breast, as if it belonged to her, as if she meant to keep it. Helga wouldn't have thought twice about keeping the butterfly. If she'd been Helga she would have laughed at the old woman for giving away a two hundred thousand dollar piece for just two hundred, and insisted the brooch was hers

Richard looked her up and down:

"Superb! La belle dame sans merci!

Her head spun. Twice in the space of a week! Richard read poetry too, just like Greg! Except Greg's belle dame sans merci was an innocent maiden, Richard's was merciless indeed.

The meal passed in a shimmer of candlelight and champagne.

The made desultory conversation. She hardly knew what she was saying. She wasn't going to sleep with him. She'd made up her mind to say yes to Greg's proposal, but at times, across the white, starched tablecloth, the things she and Richard were saying to one another felt more intimate and tender than any words a husband and wife would ever share, tenser than any exchange on their wedding night.

At other times their conversation turned harsh and coarse like words two lovers might breathe wrestling in the throes of violent lust. Thank God they were only words.

Richard looked at his watch.

"Time for bed."

"Yes." she said.

The Maha Raja Suite? There had to be a sofa or a divan or something as well as the bed.

Richard summoned a lift. The brass doors rolled open. She stepped into the lift with him.

Another mirror. Geraldine looked at herself as they rose upwards.

Richard was right. She looked superb. She felt superb. Even the fin-de-siecle brooch on her chic bandeau bodice looked just right.

CHAPTER SEVENTEEN

GERALDINE

Richard shut the door behind them and crossed the room. He parted the curtains and stood looking out across the ocean. For a moment he seemed tentative, almost shy.

He belonged to Helga. Helga was a dictator with staff and other inferiors, one she could only guess at what she'd do to hold onto this stunningly powerful man

Geraldine looked round. Yes. She'd been right. The room was furnished in palatial style. There were sofas and divans and gilt-scrolled armchairs. And a bed, with an embroidered oriental cover.

She counted the hours since Greg walked into the shop with the butterfly brooch neatly wrapped up in pink wrapping paper. Nine this morning till... after midnight... one two three four... fifteen hours since she'd readied herself to accept Greg as her husband. And now...

... Even Richard seemed daunted... he was scared of losing Helga... unless he was scared of something even more disastrous than losing Helga...?

Her lips met his, warm and sudden, sloughing off the past, stripping away everything she'd ever known or done, leaving her tongue free to grapple with the strong muscle in his mouth.

It wasn't real. This was how angels' mouths must feel when they batten on the sons of man, seraphic tongues grappling, in his mouth or hers she couldn't tell. All she knew was that the powerful meat filling her mouth was his and no one else's.

She was glad he'd chosen such a short skirt. The chiffon slid up easily over her hips, his fingers kneading the voluptuous softness of her butt through sensible cotton, clutching her pussy tight against his stiffening cock.

She wanted to say 'I love you', but 'I love you' was too weak. 'I love you' didn't convey what was pounding in her chest. She said:

"You forgot the lingerie."

He laughed in delight, a thief's hilarity.

"So I did!"

He slid his fingers under the elastic of the sensible white panties she'd put on this morning under her jeans when she thought she was dressing for Greg.

Warm palms closed round her naked butt. Strong fingers plowed her steep, tight cleft, felt the wetness spreading upwards from the pulsing ache he clutched against his stiffening dick.

He dragged her panties down around her knees with a single tug. She stepped out of sensible cotton, her high heels frantic to tread it into the floor.

She kissed his throat.

"So you think you're going to sleep with me, eh?"

His breath came in deep, heavy drafts.

"I'm sure I am."

"Is that so?"

"Mm. In fact, I'm going to fuck you stupid."

She smiled.

"I'm stupid already, doing this with you!"

"Maybe."

He unzipped her at the back.

"Hey! What do you think you're doing?"

He was unfastening her bonds. He was peeling her bandeau bodice down over her arms, away from her breasts. He gazed at where her nipples stood taut and erect in their areolae of tender pink skin.

He stooped and took her one between his teeth. A moan rose up inside her. His bite was gentle yet somehow savage too. His tongue bathed her trapped nub in delicious wetness and she moaned out loud.

"... Yes... oh yes..."

Her hand stroked his cock through his pants. It was rock hard and achingly tall. Her palm closed round his shaft through expensive fabric.

She wanted it. She needed to have his cock inside her. She'd wanted this from the very first day he'd walked into the shop.

She unzipped his pants, his tongue wrecking her mouth, holding onto his cock as her lips plastered his, holding on to him, a mast in a storm to which her whole being was lashed, a hot ocean surging in her pussy.

"... Fuck me... Richard, please... I want you to fuck me..."

He lay her down across the bed. She could feel how much he wanted to throw her down roughly, drag her legs apart, savage her, but he did it gently.

The dress was up around her waist already, her legs were spread wide already. She needed him. She needed him more than she'd ever needed anything in her whole life.

He pulled her bodice down into a ruck of black chiffon around her waist.

"... I need your cock inside me, Richard... quickly... I want your cock inside me now..."

He took his time taking his clothes off. His body was ripped and powerful. He enjoyed teasing her with his muscular beauty and the knowledge that it would soon press down on her and overwhelm her.

She fingered her clit as she watched him undress. She didn't care if this was the only time he took her. It didn't matter if he'd never fuck her again, and this was her one and only chance at ecstasy. She needed him now. He said he loved her. It wasn't important whether he meant it or not.

She smiled up at him.

"You ready yet? Gonna fuck me, Richard?"

He drew in a long powerful breath. He was trembling.

"I don't know about fuck you. I'm going to *take* you, Geraldine."

Her heart thrilled as his cock sank into her. She liked 'take'. 'Take' was even better than 'fuck'. He was taking her now, body and soul, now and forever.

"... Yes... yes... oh God... yes... yes..."

Her legs went round his hips. Her ankles raked his butt and clasped him closer as his pounding manhood filled her. Her fingernails clawed at his back. Helpless cries ached in her throat as the dam inside her burst and a deluge of delight went over her.

"... Yes... ye-eeeeeeeeeeeeeeeeeeees...!"

His lips feasted on her lips. His strong tongue blocked the delicious cries erupting in her mouth, his thick cock impaling her hard and deep again and again like he wanted to finish her off.

"... Oh God... yes... ye-eeeeeeeeeeeeeeeeeeeeeeeeeeees...!"

Her climax went on and on, carrying her far away. Her helpless gash mounted his shaft time after time taking him in deeper and deeper

She was gripped by a rhythm that had never beaten within her body before. It was his rhythm too.

The slithering moisture oiling her butt, the hot slick streaming down her thighs was his seed as much as her juice.

He'd climaxed... he must have climaxed... yet his desire didn't miss a beat, it only got stronger.

He'd given himself utterly, she'd given herself utterly, but instead of subsiding into blissful sleep—that could come later— they kept on fucking, as if both of them knew that this was their only chance.

"... I love you, Richard... I do... I love you...!"

He groaned:

"I told you already, didn't I?"

It didn't mean anything. It didn't matter if it didn't mean anything.

She was so wet and wide open for his love she thought her ecstasy must surely dissolve him into a dream, but every time she was about to awaken, Richard was there, his throbbing cock carrying her off further and deeper.

She lost count of the times she came.

He feasted on her breasts, on her throat, on her forehead, on her mouth. His hunger was savage and insatiable, yet her body kept on satisfying him, again and again, as if she were almost magic.

... For one terrible instant he was gone... a brutal disgusted withdrawal... and Geraldine went to cry out in protest except her mouth was filled with his cock and she was sucking her own juice off his shaft, and hungrily, voraciously, licking his seed from his pulsing spear-head.

He kissed her throat, her breasts, her cleavage, hungry mouth meat drilled the voluptuous dent in her belly, feasted on her quaking mound, plastered wet, black hair on her pulsing swamp... taking his time reaching the place of joy, but suddenly her helpless gash was yearning upwards for his mouth and his mouth was battening on sopping cling-film, his tongue plastering aching rhythms into her throbbing clit...

... Geraldine lost track of time. There were moments when their kisses turned to words... to sweet promises of love and dirty jibes...

... And suddenly he was inside her again, and they were moving in sync towards a consummation beyond even the most ecstatic release.

CHAPTER EIGHTEEN

GERALDINE

She woke early, curled close against his body on the luxurious softness of the hotel bed. She woke early because she was filled with so much gladness it wouldn't let her sleep any longer. Something deeply right had happened.

She knew that there were problems ahead, problems with Greg in particular, but somehow she didn't feel guilty. She hated the thought of hurting Greg, of telling him that she'd slept with Richard. But sleeping with Richard felt so necessary it was impossible for her to feel bad about it.

A warm breath caressed her ear. The warmth turned to a kiss. The kiss traveled to her mouth and she felt his hand close round her breast.

This time they made love tenderly and gently. It was hard to tell whether she mightn't still dreaming as Richard rolled on top her and her legs wrapped round his butt, drawing him in.

It was nearly lunchtime before they showered and ate in the hotel restaurant. Richard smiled:

"Shall we stay another night?"

"I can't."

"Last night was so good. Let's stay here."

Geraldine kissed him.

"I can't. There's things I need to sort out. Important things. First and foremost, Mrs Daley. I simply must return the brooch to her, Richard. And tell her how much it's worth. I feel bad leaving it so long already."

She blushed. She was only doing the right thing, what any decent person would do, but he looked at her as if she were the most generous woman in the world.

"Sure," he said. "I'll get the car."

It was a beautiful sunny day. The drive back along the cliff road was exhilarating.

By mid afternoon they were cruising into Portslade.

There was another dumpster standing outside Mrs Daley's house, filled with a new load of household detritus.

A man came out with a roll of torn lino and threw it onto the piled up floorboards and moldy plaster.

There was a FOR SALE sign nailed to the fence. For twenty four voluptuous hours she'd put it out of her mind.

The front door stood wide open. Geraldine hurried in.

"Anyone there?"

The house was being gutted. The dim rooms were stripped of their smelly carpets and tatty wallpaper.

Richard and Geraldine found the foreman.

Mrs Daley was dead. She'd died just a few days ago. In her will she'd left the entire proceeds from the sale of her house to an animal charity.

"... But... her relatives?" said Geraldine. "... Doesn't she have any relatives?"

As far as the foreman knew Mrs Daley had died without leaving any heirs or relatives behind her. They could check with the council, but no loved-ones had come forward to challenge the will, or even attend the poor old lady's funeral.

"I feel dreadful," said Geraldine. She stood there with the brooch in her hand. "What'll I do?"

Richard smiled.

"You did pay for it."

"Two hundred dollars!"

In fact, Greg had paid for it... then... Greg had given it to her... she didn't know what to do...

"I suppose you could give it to charity," said Richard. "The old lady's animal charity."

"... Yes... yes... I suppose I could do that..."

Diamonds, sapphires and emeralds beat their wings in the sun. The butterfly was so beautiful. It sparkled in her hand like a poisonous insect.

She had to get back to Clifton. God knows what had happened to Kirsty. Beth had seemed more helpful than usual but she'd left the poor girl in charge for nearly a day! And Helga was there! Helga was in Clifton!

"We'd better be getting back."

They pulled up outside Seaside Antiques And Curios.

The shutters were up. The OPEN sign in the door.

She'd misjudged Beth, the girl was an angel

Geraldine hurried in, Richard close behind her.

"Ah!" said Helga, behind the counter. "You're back!"

CHAPTER NINETEEN

Geraldine had forgotten how imposing Helga could be. Geraldine was as tall as her boss, but Helga always wore unspeakably high heels so that she could look down on everybody. She was so supermodel slim that for an instant Geraldine wondered if her own generous curves weren't somehow lacking.

Then she remembered how her shapely softness had melted in Richard's hands last night, and her heart rejoiced, even while it was beating with shock. Helga was overpowering.

"Richard!" Helga's dark cherry lips pursed. She looked from Richard to Geraldine and back again. "... Oh... I see..."

"You can see all you want, Helga," said Richard. He put his arm around Geraldine. "I don't care."

Helga's photogenic features hardened. Her cold blue eyes looked directly into Geraldine's. She studied Geraldine's cocktail dress, its Bardot bodice, the butterfly brooch. *She'd let Richard pin it back on her breast.*

"I don't like people who steal from me, Geraldine."

Geraldine didn't know if she meant the brooch or Richard.

Richard laughed lightly. He squeezed Geraldine's waist. The squeeze was warm but suddenly it didn't feel reassuring.

"Geraldine didn't steal me, Helga. I insisted on being stolen."

Helga's eyes stared daggers at Geraldine.

"You think you can steal my man?"

"Geraldine doesn't have to 'try', Helga. I love her. Geraldine has everything."

Helga's mouth twisted.

"Except a job!"

"What?"

Geraldine new the blow was coming but she still felt shocked.

"You heard me! Pack your things. You're fired!"

"But..."

She realized how much she loved her job. All the grumbling she'd done about Beth and Kirsty, and Greg too, but these five years had been the happiest of her life. She'd never find another job as good as this one. She loved her job so much she suddenly felt as if she couldn't function without it.

Richard squeezed her, but having someone's arm around you isn't always comforting. He said:

"You can't just sack her! Just because she slept with me!" His face darkened. "She's managed your shop and run your guest house perfectly. She's never let you down!"

It was nice he was standing up for her, but he was only standing up for her so she could keep her job. Helga was rich and powerful. She was beautiful. He daren't risk losing Helga for a mere manageress of a shop, a mere *ex*-manageress of a shop.

"I can do whatever I like, darling," said Helga. "I don't employ thieves."

His face flushed.

"You don't own me, Helga. I'm not your possession. Geraldine didn't *steal* me. I..."

His grip on her waist relaxed. He wavered. He was a beautiful, strong powerful man but under Helga's icy scrutiny he was wavering.

Helga's eyes glinted.

"Of course she's a thief." She rounded on Geraldine. She stared at the butterfly pulsing trembling on Geraldine's breast. "She's a light-fingered little shop girl. *What's that you're wearing?!*"

"Look, Helga..." said Richard. It was the first time that Geraldine had heard him sound uncertain, like a lost little boy.

"I sent you down here to check out business, Richard. Not fuck the staff. I've had a good look at the books. While you were enjoying your bit on the side!" Yes, that was all she was, 'a bit on the side.' "And the profits aren't anything like what they should be! I'm selling the shop!

I'm selling it right now! I've already spoken to the agent. The shop and the guest house too!"

"You can't do that," said Geraldine. "Greg..." Greg was the first thought that came to her mind. "... And Beth and Kirsty... they depend on the guest house for a living... and the shop... they'll have no money... they'll be out of work..."

Helga's eyes were icy cold:

"They can blame you for that!"

Geraldine's face burned. They would blame her too, especially Greg. Gossip about her and Richard was proably all over town by now..

"... But... that's horrible...!" She sounded like a little girl.

"Pack your things!" cried Helga. "If you're not off the premises in an hour I'm calling the police!"

Geraldine couldn't speak. She looked at Richard. He looked away.

"... I'll just... erm... see if I can't..."

He was staying. He was staying here with Helga. To talk to Helga, make his peace with her.

CHAPTER TWENTY

GREG

He was out of his job. Geraldine hadn't shown her face but she didn't need to. News of the row in the shop had reached him even down here in his workshop.

The rumors he'd heard of Richard and Geraldine driving off somewhere to spend the night together had been confirmed by the ruckus in the shop. Helga had turned up out of the blue and caught Richard with Geraldine. The guest house and shop were being sold, he'd be out of a job. It was the least of his worries.

When Geraldine appeared in the doorway Greg was ready for her. She looked around at the empty garage.

"Where's the Harley?"

"Sold it," said Greg.

"... Look... Greg..." She was hesitant. "... I've got some bad news..."

"I heard already."

"... I'm afraid Helga's selling the shop and..."

"And?"

She thought he was stupid. She thought he didn't know about her and Richard.

"... Oh... that...?" She looked wretched. "... Are you angry?"

Greg didn't know what he felt. He was certainly angry about Geraldine and Richard. He was furious. He'd loved Geraldine loyally and faithfully for five years, and she'd chosen to go off at the drop of a hat with that supercilious asshole with his expensive suit and his expensive car.

On the other hand, he'd slept with Beth. He'd fucked Beth before Geraldine fucked Richard. That evened things up. It more than evened things up. He and Geraldine were on an equal footing again.

One look at her forlorn face and he saw that dashing hunky Richard had gone hurrying back to Helga with his tail between his legs.

That much was evident, and as far as Beth went... she was an okay girl, sleeping with her had been hot,, in fact Beth had a nice side to her... but it had always only ever been Geraldine..

"... Nah..." he said. "... Not really..."

"I slept with Richard. I..."

For a second Greg thought she was going to say that she loved Richard, that she still loved him, in spite of Helga being here, but she never finished the sentence.

"Yeah. I know," he said. He ought to tell her about Beth, but he decided not to. Let her feel guilty for a while. Let her suffer. If she felt guilty it might bind her to him closer when he came round to proposing to her again.

"Well... I'm sorry if I hurt you... I really am..."

He shrugged.

"I'm okay."

"What will you do?"

"Look for another job, I guess."

He had his own house, but there weren't many jobs going in Clifton.

He looked at her.

"What will you do?"

"I'll stay at the Clifton Arms for a while, I suppose, see what happens..."

Clifton only had one hotel— besides the guest house— the Clifton Arms was a four star hotel where she knew the manager. Helga would probably be staying there too, there was nowhere else in town, but that was a cross Geraldine'd just have to bear.

Greg stared at the floor.

She was going to 'see what happens', which probably meant that she still hankered after Richard, but that ship had already been sunk.

"Yes, well..." he said. "... I guess we'll see what happens, eh?"

Ten minutes later Beth came storming into the workshop.

"Shit! Would you believe it? She's only fucking fired me! Without so much as a reason why, let alone notice!"

An unwanted weight ached between his legs. Beth was sexy when she was angry. Her nice flat belly pumped furiously between her tank top and her low-slung jeans. Her snaky hips rocked with rage under skin-tight denim. The tip of the orchid tattoo above her shaved mound pumped under the Levi button.

"Come here," said Greg.

He wrapped his arms around her. He felt genuinely sorry for her losing her job. She was going to have a harder time than him. She was an unskilled domestic worker. He at least had his mechanic's certificate.

Her zip felt as tight and angry as the rest of her pulsing against his cock. He got stiff. It wasn't a problem. Beth had it, when it came to arousing a guy.

Greg knew that he was going to propose to Geraldine again, once Richard was gone and the upheavals were over, and that this time his proposal would be accepted. He certainly wasn't going to sleep with Beth again, but her tight angry pussy grinding against this throbbing in his cock felt too nice to stop. It couldn't do any harm.

Beth was making him feel better already. It'd be good for Geraldine too, to know that she wasn't the only one who could find a bit of hot loving on the side.

Beth's hand slid skillfully up and down the aching bump in his overalls. He cupped her small, taut bottom with both hands and pulled her tighter against him. Her fingers had no option but to close around his cock and start pumping it.

"Mmmmm..."

Her breath still tasted of spearmint. They kissed long and hard rocking backwards and forwards against the work bench.

Greg drew his mouth away.

"Wanta go down the beach?"

They could find somewhere behind the rocks where he could get her clothes off and maybe even go as far as a good long finger fuck. It would make him feel better.

Beth grinned.

"Yeah. Alright."

She wasn't even angry any more.

She sat beside him in the VW, quietly chewing gum and thinking her own thoughts, whatever they were.

He pulled into the cliff car park and parked nose-in to the railing..

Geraldine was around somewhere. He didn't care if she saw him with Beth or not. It'd serve her right for hurting him. It'd make Geraldine more desperate to say yes when he proposed to her.

CHAPTER TWENTY ONE

HELGA

Helga was sitting on the balcony of her room on the top floor of the Clifton Arms when she saw the VW pull into the parking lot.

She recognized the VW immediately. It belonged to that boyfriend of Geraldine's, the hunky mechanic with the blonde hair. Greg something or other. One of her employees at the shop and guest house... *ex* employees, that is...

The VW parked nose into the railing and Geraldine's boyfriend and a girl got out. Not Geraldine. A petite slim little slip of a thing. So... Greg was into hot teens, was he...?

Helga had forgotten how ripped Geraldine's boyfriend was. He had a weightlifter's build. And that fabulous blonde hair. Hunk wasn't the word for him! Geraldine had taste.

She remembered people saying that Greg and Geraldine were going to get married. They'd been going out for ages, one of those first ever love affairs that last into a long faithful marriage.

He was with a hot looking girl, but that didn't mean anything. She'd heard that Greg had girls hitting on him all the time— it was pretty obvious why, with that build and his cute face— but everyone said that he had eyes only for Geraldine.

Helga stood up and waved.

"Greg!"

He and the girl were four stories down and about fifty meters away, but Helga had one of those commanding voices that carry a long way.

"Greg! Greg!"

He turned and looked up at the balcony.

He knew who she was. They'd met on a few occasions. Helga didn't even have to shout. She understood that— tall, slim, commandingly photogenic in her six inch heels— even at this distance she stood out.

She waved for him to come up. His ex-employer, any number of positions at her fingertips to offer a skilled man, she signaled for him to come up.

He came. He said something to the girl then walked back towards the hotel. He crossed the road and stopped on the sidewalk outside the entrance, looking up.

"About your job!" Even from four stories up, she saw his eyes widen and a nice grin spread across his handsome features. She pointed at the hotel entrance. "Room Forty One."

A minute or so later there was a knock on the door. She called: "Come in."

The door opened.

Helga caught her breath. God, Geraldine sure knew how to pick them! This guy was built! From the ground up he was one ripped specimen of pure male eye candy.

She never usually went for working class men. She liked her bit of rough to be suave and sophisticated, but something about Greg really got to her. It wasn't just his chiseled features, or the biceps packed under his overalls. He was six one or so three of raw male muscle, but there was also an innocence in his blue eyes that appealed to something predatory inside her.

Or maybe it was just the fact that he was Geraldine's boyfriend that made her feel a shiver of desire.

"Sit down...?"

"Greg."

"That's right... Greg.... do take a seat."

He perched awkwardly on the edge of a sofa. She remained standing, her back straight as a ramrod. She looked at her best standing. Especially in the skin-tight black slacks Richard had peeled off so skillfully in the airport hotel, fuck him.

"Greg. I'm sorry about what's happened... you losing your job and everything... I deeply regret it."

He stared at the carpet.

"Yeah, well..."

He was gorgeously tongue tied.

"I want you to know that it isn't my fault that the shop and guest house have to close."

He shrugged, but said nothing.

"It's that bitch, Geraldine' fault."

She waited for him to protest. He didn't, he just stared at the floor.

"Never-the-less, there may be a way I can be of some assistance to you, Greg." He examined the pattern on the carpet. "I might be able to find a far better position for you than the one you've lost."

He looked up at her.

Surely he must know by now what she was suggesting. Richard would have picked up her meaning in an instant from four stories down on the sidewalk. Greg just looked cutely uncertain.

She mentioned a few of the businesses she owned, the various mechanical and engineering jobs she had at her disposal. The money they paid was much better than the shop.

He stared at her, a fraction wary, and said:.

"... So... what... what have I got to do...?"

He was quite bright, after all. He'd finally sussed the situation.

She raised an eyebrow, gave the hint of a shrug. Her glossy lips formed a questioning moue.

"Well..."

She stood in front of him, swaying ever so slightly on her stiletto heels. It was lucky Greg was tall too. When he drew in a deep breath and sat up straight on the edge of the sofa, his gorgeous face was on an exact level with her split.

"Unbutton me, Greg... that's the first thing you can do... then you can pull my zip down..."

He reached out and did what he was told. His fingers were wonderfully strong, there was a rim of grease under each nail. He tugged at her zip, his oily knuckles grazing her silk panties, as he drew it down. La Perla. She hoped he realized how expensive they were.

Helga swayed slightly towards him, her slacks gaping, and his awkward knuckles sinking deeper into the shiny fabric and the aching flesh beneath.

He paused. He knew he wasn't allowed to say anything more. Further questions were off limits. She was the one who was going to do all the talking.

"... Okay... good... now you can pull my slacks down...!" His fingernails felt wonderfully rough and strong, burrowing under her waistband. "... Take your time!"

He was breathing heavily, having a bit of trouble controlling himself. He peeled skintight cotton down over her perfect butt. Callused fingertips registered how toned and shapely her ass was. A frisson of delight shivered up her thighs. She felt like a butterfly being stripped of its chrysalis by an elephant.

She stepped out of her shoes and he pulled her slacks free.

She nodded at her foot.

He knew what she meant. He knelt and lifted her foot, cupped her heel in both hands and licked her toes. He stuffed all five of her toes into his mouth and sucked and gobbled. A hot slick prickled her pussy. These strong, warm lips had kissed Geraldine's mouth.

"... You're good, Greg... very good... I might well be able to find you a position in my own house... chauffeur, perhaps... or something even better..."

His tongue massaged her ankle. Strong mouth meat moved slowly up her inner calf. He kissed the inside off her knee. His mouth tracked the toned ascent of her inner thigh.

"... Mm... or perhaps even my personal trainer..."

He pulled her panties aside and she let his tongue plow the moist furrow of her pussy. He did it just how she liked, spreading her engorged lips with the flat of his tongue like a little boy licking an ice cream, his tongue-tip searching for her clit in a slather of sudden wetness.

Her butt kicked.

"... Oh... I like to keep in shape... I like... oh... oh-hhhhhhhhhhhhhh... "

His big hands closed round her bottom and he drove his tongue into her. He was good. He was better than Richard. She'd teach that bitch for stealing Richard.

His hands slid up under her blouse. Chapped fingertips crushed lace and elastic into the aching tightness of her nipples.

"... Or maybe even my bodyguard..."

The chains and shackles were in her suitcase, her spreader and O-ring. His overalls didn't have a belt. It wasn't a problem. She'd brought her knout and her cat o' nine tails too. They were better than Richard's belt any day... but no... not yet... his chest was heaving...she didn't want to freak the poor dear...

Helga laughed out loud:

"... It's a twenty four seven position... you'll need to be on call at any time of the day or night..."

Hurting Geraldine felt even better than hurting herself. Her laughter turned to a long low animal moaning.

What was happening? Usually she didn't like to touch a man too much, except in the area where the action was. Her fingers were clenched in a tangle of blonde hair, dragging his face harder into her pussy begging his tongue to find her melting hole.

Buttons popped. There was a tearing sound. Her blouse was around her elbows. She preferred to be chained when she controlled a man. A blouse tangled round her elbows would just have to do.

"... And fuck me whenever I tell you to..."

He dragged his mouth away from its succulent feast. The look of confusion in his eyes was delicious.

"Now?"

She only gave commands, but this one came out as a groan: "Now!"

She didn't need chains or shackles. Knowing that she was about to fuck Geraldine's boyfriend was excitement enough.

He stood up and dragged his overalls off. Her heart nearly stopped beating. His cock was tall and rock hard.

Helga fell to her knees and put it in her mouth. She'd never knelt before a man before in her whole life. It was the first time, but Greg's strong cock had sweetened Geraldine's nights, it had carried the bitch over the brink, and now it was pumping in and out of her mouth.

Her fingernails raked his butt urging him deeper. She was gagging on the stake to which Geraldine had been tied in ecstasy.

His butt kicked. The root of his cock clenched. Darling Greg was cumming.

Helga dug her fingers into his ass cheeks. His butt was quaking like a stallion's. She tried to hold him where he was. She was the one in charge.

He was too strong for her. He lifted her by her armpits and dumped her on the bed. Her legs parted helplessly.

"Yes... yes.... please.... please fuck me... please... please... fuck me hard..."

She'd never pleaded like this with a man before.

He straddled her and sank his huge tip into wet gash. She'd never been taken like this before, like a toy being pierced and destroyed. She preferred to be in control, but his cock was unforgiving, his pounding piston rammed deep inside her and next minute she was riding him, rutting Geraldine's stud with every cell in her body.

"... Yes... yes... oh God... yes... ye-eeeeeeeeeeeeeeeeeeeees...!"

Her back arched. Her butt lifted off the bed in answering ecstasy as Greg unloaded inside her. The warm hot love that had filled Geraldine filled her and turned deliciously slippery trickling down her bottom.

CHAPTER TWENTY TWO

GERALDINE

Geraldine didn't know where to go. Her bags were packed. She'd boxed up her few belongings to be sent on later to... wherever... she didn't know...

She'd dedicated the last five years of her life to Helga's Seaside Antiques And Curios and Helga's Seaside Guest House, and now suddenly she had no home.

She couldn't stay on in the Clifton Arms. The Clifton Arms was hideously expensive, and Helga's room was up on the fourth floor, plus the hotel was directly opposite the cliffside carpark where Beth and her friends hung around and she'd even caught a glimpse of Greg's VW parked near the railing.

Her parents were dead. The little money they'd left her was long spent. She didn't have much money in the bank.

Part of her wanted to stay on in Clifton, somewhere, anywhere—just not the Clifton Arms— and hopefully see Richard again. A crazy hope urged her to hang around in town till she saw Richard one more time and knew what Richard had decided, her or Helga.

There were moments when she remembered the way Richard had put his arm around her waist when Helga confronted her. She recalled, over and over, the night they'd spent together in the Belvedere in Rose Bay. Surely the ecstasy they'd shared meant Richard loved her. Surely he too knew that what they'd shared together was precious, that they were meant for each other, and, no matter how difficult the wrench from Helga might be, he wanted her.

There were other times when she recalled the bitter fact that he'd stayed behind in the shop to talk to Helga. He'd chosen to stay and argue with Helga rather than following her as she went to pack. He was Helga's boyfriend. Geraldine knew that he and Helga weren't married, but they could well have been partners for even longer than she and Greg.

And then there was the consideration of money and the celebrity lifestyle. Richard had a fortune of his own. But in this world, fortunes stick with fortunes, and Helga's wealth was even greater than his. Richard wouldn't dare sacrifice his lavish New York life for the manageress of a seaside antiques...unemployed *ex* manageress... Jobs were hard to get down on this part of the coast.

Part of her wanted to wait in Clifton so she could see Richard again. But that was the weak, clinging part of her, the dumped, dependent girly part, hanging around in case her man had a change of heart.

No. She'd be better off out of Clifton, especially after what she'd done to Greg. Seeing Greg again was the last thing she wanted. Bumping into him in main street, or down by the beach, would be more than she could bear.

There was a hotel in Portslade, Mrs Daley's town, that was clean and cheap. And Geraldine had business in Portslade, something she needed to sort out. In fact, she wouldn't really rest until she'd sorted it out.

She took a bus along to the next town and found a cheap place to stay.

Over the next three weeks Geraldine combined looking for jobs— unsuccessfully— with trying to find Mrs Daley's surviving family, to give them the brooch. She felt like a thief, as long as she held onto the butterfly without giving it back to its rightful owners. She'd cheated the old woman, giving her two hundred dollars for something that was worth one hundred and fifty five thousand.

She went to council offices and estate agents and the registrar of births and deaths. She wouldn't sleep till the Fabergé brooch was back where it belonged.

****

Greg mooned round Clifton for three whole weeks without seeing either Geraldine or Beth. The money he'd got for the Harley was running out. He applied for jobs, but there were currently no positions vacant for mechanics in the area.

The glittering promises of a well-paid job that Helga had made to him proved to be empty. The fantastic positions he'd been assured he would get had turned out to be merely a means to lure him into bed. He'd been used and then dumped.

Actually, he hadn't need much luring, which made him feel even worse. Helga had been hot in bed, but she'd disappeared almost immediately after the two of them had fucked their brains out. Greg guessed that he was too coarse and common for Helga.

He'd turned up at Helga's hotel the next morning, as much for another shot at her, if truth be told, as for a job, and she'd already checked out and left.

He didn't even see Beth around town. In a way, he missed her. Beth talked rude and she was too loose in her ways with men, but she wasn't a bad kid underneath it. She was nicer than Helga, that was for sure. She was sexier than Helga too, in her own way, even though she didn't have Helga's expensive clothes and sophisticated manner. He would have liked to see her, but Beth had disappeared from the scene too.

Greg didn't even like to think about Geraldine. He'd lost Geraldine, and he knew it. He tried to block her out of his mind. Thinking about her hurt too much.

****

It was a Friday evening. Greg sat in the cliff car park, in his VW, looking out over the ocean. The sun was going down on the horizon, painting the sea orange and gold.

Up on main street the neon lights were getting brighter as night came on. It was nice just sitting here, looking at the sunset, but he was going to have to sell the VW soon. Then he'd have nowhere to sit and think.

He decided to go up to where the lights were, and get drunk.

Suddenly the door opened. It was Beth. She slipped into the passenger seat beside him. The gear stick rattled as she climbed between Greg and the steering wheel and straddled him.

"Where...?"

Her lips were hot and sinuous, snaking across his mouth, searching for his tongue. She tasted of spearmint. There was a melting feeling in the back of his throat as he gave his mouth to her.

Her fingers raked his hair, clutched and dragged his tongue deeper.

He wanted to ask her where she'd been. He needed to know what had happened to her, but she wouldn't let him speak.

A sharp heat came from between her legs, straight through her skintight jeans. She refused to let go of him with her mouth as she lifted herself and freed his cock from his jeans.

He heard her zip sliding down. Suddenly her jeans were around her knees. The steering wheel banged as she kicked them off.

Before he knew what was happening she'd impaled herself on him. A desperate heat enveloped his aching manhood. Her spine beat time on the steering wheel as her pussy jerked backwards and forwards on his aching stiffness.

Her wet gash came undulating over him, riding him with sweet young heat. Helga was nothing next to her. Helga was dead as a piece of stone compared to Beth's eager juiciness slithering on his plastered bush.

His cock clenched and kicked inside her. For such a thin, whippy body Beth was voluptuously wet.

All he could do was hold onto her butt and feel how nice she was, how generous her snaking love for him was.

"... Where...?"

His question turned to a groan as a wave of ecstasy lifted both of them off the seat, her knees holding him tight as he exploded inside her.

He stroked her hair as she lay panting on his chest. He ran his fingers through a spiky peroxide hairdo.

"Shit..." He whispered. "... That's the second time we've forgotten to use a condom..."

He felt too satisfied to really worry.

She grinned. Her breath was hot in his ear.

"Don't need a condom no more, Greg."

"Eh?"

"You n me. We don't need to use a condom from now on..."

"Now on?"

She gazed almost fiercely into his eyes.

"... Do you love me, Greg...?" He didn't know what to say. "... I hope so...'cause I'm pregnant."

CHAPTER TWENTY FOUR

Geraldine went back to her room. She stood at the window and looked out over the ocean. The room was basic. The mattress of her double bed was hard, but the view made up for a lot.

She'd tried to keep herself busy, searching for a job and hunting for the rightful owners of the flamingo brooch, to block out the pain of losing Richard. She missed him dreadfully, but he was obviously back in New York now, living with Helga. He'd probably already forgotten about the night they'd spent together.

It was evenings like this, coming back to her room, looking out over the ocean with an empty night ahead of her, that the pain was at its worst. The night of passion they'd shared had been magical, their ecstasy something special, yet he'd turned his back on it and gone back to Helga.

No doubt Helga had her own ways of holding onto him. Helga was bossy and manipulative. She no doubt knew all sorts of tricks in bed, sex games that Geraldine couldn't even dream of, to make Richard love her. If only she'd known what Helga had, when it came to sex, that she didn't have.

Geraldine looked at the sparse hotel bed with its plain white cover. It was too early to try and sleep. A walk along the beach might buck her up.

She kicked off her shoes, and took her tights off. She slipped out of the business suit she wore for job interviews and put on a beach wrap. It was a hot night and the thin cotton felt cool and light on her aching limbs.

****

Walking along the wet sand felt nice. Occasionally a larger wave broke on the beach and the shore wash ran over her ankles. Geraldine headed

117

for the rocks on the point where the sun was going down. It was a long walk but she finally reached the point. Then she headed back.

By the time she got back to her room it was dark. She opened the door of her room and sank down onto the bed. She was too tired and lonely to even bother switching the light on.

For an instant she didn't see Richard standing by the window.

"Richard!"

His dark eyes shone in the light of the moon.

"I've found you," he said.

She was in his arms. There were so many things she needed to say, but his lips were feasting on hers like a starving man's feasting on meat. There were so many questions she needed to ask him, but her tongue was too hungry for his tongue.

He'd come for her. They'd never part again. She knew it with all her heart and soul. She was his and he was hers. It ought to have been a romantic moment. It should have been a night for murmuring sweet nothings and for dreamy words, but he was already unfastening her wrap.

His hands were exploring her body as if he only had seconds to live and he needed to touch every inch of her before he died.

Her hands were no different. She was unfastening buttons, clawing at his zip. His cock filled her palm. It was so tall and hard, just wrapping her fingers around it made her pussy melt. Her leg lifted and twined round his waist hastening him to get inside her before she came.

His hands clutched her butt and lifted her against him. Her panties were gone. His fingers plowed the cleft of her ass and felt the wetness rising from between her legs.

"I love you, Geraldine..."

"Yes. Yes."

God! How strong he was! His hands were cupped round her bottom lifting her, lifting her high, all the way up to the tip of his cock, the tip of his cock taut with desire, quivering with tenderness, sinking between the molten folds of her desperation.

She wrapped her other leg around him. He bore her weight as she sank around him. Her pussy was already kicking before it had reached the bottom of its perilous descent. Her butt was already bucking. She was already riding a wave of ecstasy as he impaled her.

The orgasm ran over her like hot water bathing her from head to toe, her heart wanting him to cum and begging him not to. She needed more. She needed so much more.

Her bottom was slipping and sliding in her own juice, she begged him in her heart to climax, not to climax. She didn't want to mix this delicious slipperiness with his hot seed yet. She had to know everything. She needed to know him through and through.

"How does Helga do it?"

"Eh?"

His eyes gazed into hers, baffled.

"You heard me. What do you do with Helga?"

The most swashbuckling grin that she'd ever seen, a pirate's loving smile, buckled his broad lips.

"Helga?"

"Yes. Helga."

"You sure?"

"I'm sure."

He laid her gently on the bed on her back. She stayed impaled on his cock as her body spread across the mattress. She groaned out loud as he pulled out.

"Close your eyes."

She did what she was told.

She felt one of her wrists being bound tightly in... hang on...!... that lacy silk was her panties!... he stretched her arm out as far as it would go and strapped her wrist to something hard and smooth... the bedpost!

Her body was still arching and writhing in ecstasy from the climax he'd just given her.

"Other arm!"

She stretched her other arm out as far as it would go. She heard a fizz of nylon. It was deliriously tight, going round her wrist. He was strapping her other arm to the other bedpost with her stockings.

"Spread your legs."

Her butt kicked. She was cumming again. She couldn't help it. Her body went into overdrive, hearing that note of command in his voice, the hint of danger she'd heard the very first time he walked into the shop.

"Keep still!"

She felt the thin cotton of her wrap being fastened around her ankle. It jerked her legs even wider open. She felt a moment's awe at Helga's knowledge of men and her skill with sex. But the awe was swept away by a wave of exultation. Love is more powerful than skill or even knowledge.

"Fuck me, Richard. Please. Now. I want you to fuck me."

Her need was too urgent. She couldn't even make out what he tied her other ankle with.

The bed creaked. The mattress sank. He was kneeling between her legs, but she still kept her eyes shut.

In the darkness his cock felt even bigger than the first time, its stillness even more ecstatic as her frantic need enfolded it. Her back arched and drove him inwards. She wanted him in all the way. She wanted him in deep, deeper than he'd ever been before.

He touched her clit, and she exploded in another orgasm.

His fingertip circled on her clit. She could feel how much he loved her and wanted her, just in the gentle churning of one fingerprint over her pulsing nub.

"I love you, Geraldine."

"... Yes... yes..."

She yearned to throw her arms around him and feel his lips on hers. She needed to wrap her legs around him and force him deeper with her heels but she couldn't. Her body bucked and jerked, but she still couldn't reach him.

Geraldine didn't believe in magic, but when he wrapped his arms around her quaking shoulders and gave himself to her, something magical happened. She was flat on her back, bound hand and foot, and yet it was as if she had spirit arms and spirit legs, and her spirit body bent upwards from the waist and invicle thighs clamped his hips and invisible arms went round his neck and they embraced him and their bodies became one.

Her tailbone was double jointed fucking his fathomless thrusts, orgasm after orgasm. His hot seed filled her. It spilled out of her, and streamed down her bottom and trickled onto the bedspread, but he still didn't stop. He couldn't stop. He was fucking her from the bottom of his heart and she was responding to every thrust.

It seemed as if nothing would ever satisfy him, and yet his eyes brimmed an amazed fulfillment as he ravished her.

There were moments when it felt as if it would go on forever, but at last they lay, panting and satisfied, in each others' arms.

CHAPTER TWENTY FIVE

"I don't know what to do with it, Richard," said Geraldine. "I feel bad keeping it."

The butterfly brooch sat on the dressing table. They were getting ready to leave for New York.

The glitter that was real diamonds, not glass, caught a ray of sunlight and sparkled like a rainbow. Just looking at the brooch made her feel guilty. She was dressed in a new, chic suit that Richard had bought her, but she was reluctant to pin the butterfly to her lapel.

He kissed her.

"Go on. Put it on. It's beautiful, and so are you."

"But it's worth so much money! And I only gave that poor woman two hundred dollars."

It was still gnawing at her.

Richard looked at his watch.

"Come on, Geraldine! It's time to go!" He added a touch of authority to his tone. "Put it on!"

"Oh... okay..."

She let him pin the brooch to her jacket. He smiled:

"Let's hit the road!"

So many exciting things lay ahead of her. First, a trip to Europe. A holiday in Paris, Rome and Greece, to relax after the difficulties of the last month. Then her new job in New York, working as Richard's personal assistant and manager of the marketing company he'd recently asquired. Then, settling into their Central Park apartment. And last but not least, a wedding and starting a family.

"There's one more thing, Richard."

It was a lot to look forward to, but Geraldine couldn't leave Clifton in a happy state if she didn't have a completely clear conscience.

"Oh... and what's that?"

"I want to say goodbye to Greg."

She studied his face for signs of jealousy. No. Richard wasn't one to be jealous of any man in existence.

"You think that's a good idea?"

Perhaps he *was* jealous. He sensed how deeply committed she'd been to Greg, and how bad she felt about hurting Greg.

She wanted to say goodbye to Greg more as a way of apologizing for letting him down than just to say goodbye. But maybe Richard was right. Going to see Greg was a bad idea.

She smiled at the gorgeous man whom she loved and who loved her.

"Oh. Okay. Let's hit the road!"

Richard drove slowly along Main Street, letting her have one last look at the town before she said goodbye to it.

The traffic lights turned red, and he halted behind a truck. Geraldine cried out:

"Oh!"

Greg was walking along the sidewalk no more than two meters away, dressed in his usual overall. He was with a girl. In fact he was with Beth! They were walking along together... and Greg had his arm around Beth's shoulder!

The lights changed to green. Richard began to pull away.

"Wait!"

Geraldine flung her door open and jumped out of the car. The cars behind Richard were already blowing their horns. Richard had to pull in to the curb.

Richard didn't get out. He sat and waited.

Geraldine was on the sidewalk, talking to Greg and to a particularly pretty girl in a yellow sundress.

Far from looking angry and resentful as he spoke to Geraldine, Greg's face was animated with an obvious pride and delight. The girl was talking to Geraldine too. At last Richard remembered who she was.

It was that girl Beth who used to work in the guest house. Richard remembered her as a surly looking little slut, but now her expression was as sunny as her dress.

She even reached up and gave Geraldine a kiss. Geraldine was giving Beth something. Geraldine's back was turned to the street. Richard couldn't see what it was that Geraldine was doing.

Geraldine shook hands with Greg, then kissed him too.

When she climbed back into the car, her face was radiant.

Richard glanced at her lapel.

"Hey! Where's your brooch?"

Geraldine smiled. He'd never seen her look so pleased.

"Oh!" she said airily, waving back at the couple on the sidewalk. "It's only an old brooch. Come on! Let's go!"

Also by Clea Jones

Between a Cop and a Hard Place
The Hooker Next Door
Hard Man, Soft Fan
Geraldine's Taken

9 798223 358756